PILLOW TALK

Journalist Sorrel Elliot's relationship with Matt Ramirez, one of the world's richest bachelors, began as a strictly between-the-sheets investigation — until she fell in love with him. But when he discovered her true identity, Sorrel lost both the story and the man! Five years on, she runs into Matt in Barbados — the last place on earth she had expected. Now, two things remain constant — their heady attraction for one another, and Matt's suspicious mind!

REBECCA KING

PILLOW TALK

Complete and Unabridged

LINFORD
Leicester

First published in Great Britain in 1995

First Linford Edition
published 2007

All the characters in this book have no existence
outside the imagination of the author, and have
no relation whatsoever to anyone bearing the
same name or names. They are not even
distantly inspired by any individual known
or unknown to the author, and all the incidents
are pure invention.

British Library CIP Data

King, Rebecca
    Pillow talk.—Large print ed.—
Linford romance library
    1. Love stories
    2. Large type books
    I. Title
    823.9'14 [F]

    ISBN 978–1–84617–829–0

Published by
F. A. Thorpe (Publishing)
Anstey, Leicestershire

Set by Words & Graphics Ltd.
Anstey, Leicestershire
Printed and bound in Great Britain by
T. J. International Ltd., Padstow, Cornwall

This book is printed on acid-free paper

For Figaro and Charlie —
staunchest of friends

Prologue

Once more, in that dream, she was on a beach. Under the pale tropical moonlight the sand was a strange, unearthly silver, and it was soft under her bare feet. The sea was rough — she could hear its dull booming and see, far out, the wall of breakers crawling endlessly towards her.

She walked down to that dark line where the sea met the land. As she knelt the water foamed over her nakedness, patterning her flesh like white lace, and gradually she sank down in it. Beyond the reef the waves were still thundering, and a line of white sea-horses were racing to the shore. They seemed to rear themselves up over her, the opaque gleam on the underwave glinting like metal as the moon's rays caught it.

Then, as she watched spellbound, he came — as he always did. The water parted and one of those sea-horses came plunging through, straight as an arrow towards her. There was no time for fear; the horse was almost on her before she saw, low on its back, fingers twined in the flying mane, the dark rider.

The horse reared, then halted almost at her feet and stood, tossing its head and snorting as the spray broke round it. The rider sat, looking silently down at her where she lay at his feet, then dismounted, throwing the reins over the stallion's back. He stood over her, his body gleaming silver, his face — as always — hidden by his mount's arching neck.

The blood was roaring in her ears, drowning the crash of breakers, as she held out her arms to him. Then, as he came down to her, his face moved from shadow into moonlight. And — as always — she woke . . .

1

'More champagne, *señorita*?'

'No thank you, Jorge.'

As Sorrel replaced her empty glass on the silver tray which the manservant was holding out to her she glanced across the room, through the animated groups of grey-suited men and elegantly dressed women, towards Matt. He was deep in conversation with a grey-haired man — her keen ears just caught the deep velvety timbre of his voice, with that husky, slightly foreign inflexion — but, as if sensing her eyes on him, his head turned sharply and a quick, conscious look passed between them before he turned back to his companion.

That snatched look, full of tenderness and more — a sharp, physical awareness — made her pulses leap, her breathing quicken. Tonight, she knew with instant, absolute certainty, Matt was going to ask her to stay with him. And, with equal certainty, she knew that she would.

Terrified that the peony colour rising in her normally pale cheeks would betray the sudden blaze of emotion, she turned away to the huge picture window. The view from Matt's penthouse was, if anything, even more spectacular by night than by day. Half of London was bathed in a soft glow, while at her feet the River Thames slid past, its opaque surface puckered by the raindrops which gave the scene a misty, luminous quality, so that every streetlight across the bridge to her right had blossomed into a tiny golden chrysanthemum.

It was raining harder now, the drops trickling down the pane. Like tears, she thought, then half smiled at the fancy. There would be no tears tonight. She would give herself to Matt willingly, joyfully, because she loved him.

When had it happened, that final step on the path from suspicion and hostility to unwilling attraction for a handsome, sexually alluring male and on across the shadowy frontier into the first passionate love of her nineteen years?

She knew when — just a few hours ago. Strolling hand in hand through St James's Park on their way back to his apartment, they'd stopped to feed the ducks. In the same instant they'd turned to look at each other, laughing over a couple of squabbling drakes, and something had flickered in his pale green eyes. The intensity of their gaze had held them locked in a private world for long seconds; London had receded to a million miles away. Then a joy so exquisite that it had almost been pain filled her, and a feeling of such rapture that even now it was surely air she trod beneath her feet, and not the soft Chinese silk rug.

And yet, little more than three weeks ago she'd never even heard of Mateo Ramirez . . .

'Head of the Bank of Tierranueva, just about the biggest merchant bank in

Central America, aged thirty, unmarried, but an eye — and plenty more, if a quarter of the talk about him is true — for a pretty face. And that's where you come in, Sorrel, sweetie.'

'How do you mean, Bryden?'

She'd looked up abruptly from her doodle-pad. It had been the first time in this highly-charged meeting that he'd addressed her directly, and, although she hoped it didn't show, she still felt very much the new girl in the team. She'd been taken on just a few weeks previously, and was still counting her luck at having broken through to a national newspaper so early in her journalistic career.

All right, so maybe the *Planet* wasn't the most highly-regarded paper ever, at least, in intellectual circles. But its Bryden Tarre 'Insider' column had a widely envied — and feared — reputation for its hard-hitting exposures of wrong-doings in high places, and she was proud to be a member of its background research team.

'As I said, an eye for a pretty face. We may have hired you as a computer wizard, Sorrel, but I hope there's no hurt feelings — ' Bryden had glanced smilingly around the oval table ' — if I say that yours is the prettiest face we've got.'

She had looked at him uncertainly. 'But — what exactly do you have in mind?'

'Pillow talk — that's what I have in mind, darling.'

'Oh, no. I'm sorry, Bryden, but — ' She'd half risen from her chair, the agitated colour flooding her cheeks.

'But nothing.' His voice had hardened a fraction. 'Look, Sorrel, you agree that if the allegations against Ramirez hold up we've got our biggest exposé ever?'

'Yes — '

'And you also agree that if that smooth bastard really is using his bank as a front for laundering drugs money, then he needs nailing — and by any means?'

'Yes, of course. It's a filthy trade, but — '

'By any means.' Bryden had overridden her remorselessly. 'Dave following up London contacts, Rik and Jason at the sharp end out in Tierranueva, and you. All I'm asking you to do, for God's sake, is sleep with the guy . . . '

She hadn't, of course, though the attraction had been there right from day one — that first engineered meeting — like a sudden spark of high-voltage electricity. Wholly inexperienced though she was, she'd recognised that mutual undercurrent tug of sexuality, even though at first he'd been formal, almost aloof sometimes, in his attitude to her — quite at odds with the lurid picture that Bryden had painted of him.

But then, a few nights ago, after driving her back to her flat from a trip to the theatre, he'd taken her in his arms and kissed her until she was mindblown, only able to cling helplessly to him, arching her neck with a tiny moan as his lips had fastened on the crazily beating pulse at its base. He'd released her just as abruptly, though, and when she'd shyly asked him in for a coffee, he'd given her a rather lopsided smile.

'I think maybe that would not be too wise, little one.' And since then he'd gone back to his formal correctness, only kissing her hand, though even that — the brush of his lips against her palm — was enough to set every pulse in her body on fire . . .

Reflected in the rain-streaked window, she gazed at herself. The short pink silk dress — which Matt, despite her protests, had insisted on buying for his party tonight — clung to her slender figure, and her hair, the colour of pale wheat under the subtle lights, was piled on her head in what she'd thought was a sophisticated chignon until she'd seen some of the other women arrive. The delicate oval of her face, and her eyes, darker in that blurred image than the reality of soft sapphire, were glowing with naked emotion for the whole world to see.

In the mirrored throng behind her she glimpsed Matt and the other man, still engrossed in conversation. They both seemed to be looking at her and she turned, a self-conscious little smile on her lips. Matt's eyes, though, as they met hers, were remote — but that was Matt. He was single-minded — ruthless, even — in business matters, and she knew that he was able to lose himself entirely in whatever he was doing — and right now high finance was no doubt uppermost in his mind.

But she was quite sure that he was honest. Oh, she had no proof, but every instinct told her that this man whom she loved would never get himself involved with any criminal activities. And she'd tell Bryden so tomorrow — at the same time as telling him that she was leaving the team. Maybe when she was older . . . But now she simply wasn't cut out for tough work like this. She just hoped that her boss's probing mind wouldn't pick up the pathetic truth — that she'd fallen headlong in love with her quarry.

Love . . . She gave a wry little smile. She'd certainly been behaving like a lovelorn adolescent earlier today. Left alone in the apartment, while Matt was at a meeting and Jorge had taken himself off to have his immaculate black hair barbered, she'd mooned about — first into Matt's dressing-room, to rearrange his silver-backed hairbrushes, then, as her heart had beaten erratically, she had peeped into his bedroom, with its king-size bed, before finding herself in his study.

Absently she'd picked up one of the computer disks arranged in a neat row on his desk, then paused, chewing on her underlip. If she fed these into the computer, she'd thought, maybe she could at least tell Bryden that there was nothing incriminating in his personal files . . . She had half slotted it in, but then — no, they had been personal, *private*.

As she had withdrawn it she'd heard the key in the front door. Hastily she'd jammed the disk back into the row, and when Jorge had come into the sitting-room she'd been there, sitting on the cream leather sofa, casually flipping through a magazine, only her breathing a little flurried . . .

As she watched now, Matt put down his glass and made his way between the talking, laughing groups towards her, moving with that lazy panther-like grace that she was coming to know so well. How handsome he was — his black hair and lean, saturnine face set off by the white shirt and the midnight-blue jacket, while the charcoal-grey trousers enhanced the long legs and narrow yet muscular haunches. And all at once the image rose in her of that same body naked, muscles rippling beneath skin which was smooth as brown satin, his eyes dark with desire as his mouth came down on hers . . .

For a second, drowning in that sensual image, she could only gaze at him wordlessly. But then, running the tip of her tongue round her soft lips, she said huskily, 'Hi.'

'Hi. Enjoying yourself?' His voice was faintly sardonic.

'Oh, yes. It's a great party, Matt.'

He laughed softly. 'Yeah. I just wish they'd all go.'

All but lost in the music and the laughter, the words were for her alone, and she felt the colour rise to her cheeks again.

Taking her hand, he raised it, turned it so that her small, pale pink palm lay across his larger, tanned one. Then, lowering his head, he kissed it. His lips scarcely brushed the skin, and yet little needle-points of electricity pricked through her veins, and when he ran his mouth along each fingertip, before gently catching the soft pad of flesh at the base of her thumb between his white teeth, a faint spasm made her whole body tremble.

'Oh, Matt,' she whispered throatily, but with a glinting smile he released her hand.

'Later, my sweet — when our

audience has left.' And he was gone.

Her stomach was lurching in a tumultuous cocktail of exhilaration, apprehension, and the richly sensual promise of unknown things, but somehow she fixed her brightest party smile in place and turned to speak to the couple nearest to her . . .

★ ★ ★

'Goodnight, Señorita Elliot.'

The last of the guests, a distinguished-looking white-haired man — one of the high-ups at the Tierranuevan Embassy, she'd gathered — took her hand, raising it to his lips in a thoroughly Latin gesture. He smiled at her, said something to Matt in Spanish, and then he had gone.

'What did he say?'

Matt closed the door. 'Oh, merely something to the effect that you're far too pretty to let slip through my fingers.'

'I see.' She smiled at him uncertainly.

'And — and will you?'

He stood looking down at her, his green eyes intent.

'Oh, no, Sorrel,' he said, a husky catch in his deep voice. 'I have no intention of doing that.'

Drawing her into his arms, he clasped her against him so that she was aware of every vibrantly male line of that strong body, and of the slight tremor which was running through it. At last he held her away from him and gazed at her, all the hard lines of his face softened into tenderness.

'Oh, *querida*, I've waited so long — three whole weeks — ' he gave a wry little grimace ' — but tonight — it is our night, isn't it?'

Sorrel felt her love for him bubbling up into pure joy. 'Yes, please, Matt,' she whispered.

'Oh, my precious girl.'

His fingers tightened on her wrists, then, putting his arm around her, he led the way back into the sitting-room where Jorge and the two hired waitresses

15

in their neat black dresses had already all but cleared away the party debris.

'Leave the rest, Jorge — and I shan't need you again tonight,' Matt said.

The man nodded. 'Goodnight, *señor* — Señorita Elliot.'

He shepherded the two girls out, and Sorrel heard the discreet clunk as the heavy door to the kitchen quarters swung to behind them.

One of the tapes of Latin-American folk music was still playing softly — the haunting sound of reedy pipes and thin human voices heart-wrenching in its poignancy. Matt walked across to the CD-player and clicked it off, and in the sudden silence she was certain she could hear her heart fluttering against her ribs.

He took off his jacket and tie and slung them over a chair, then eased open the two top buttons of his shirt.

'A drink?' From an ice-bucket, he drew out an unopened bottle of champagne.

'No, thanks. I've had enough.' Although

all at once her mouth was dry, so that she could barely speak for wanting him.

Matt gave her a lopsided grin. 'I think maybe I have too.'

He replaced the bottle, came across to where she stood beside the marble fireplace, and, taking her in his arms again, kissed her. And now there was no more gentleness. His mouth came down against hers, and as her lips parted his tongue plunged between her teeth to thrust into her mouth, filling her with the honeyed taste of him, their mouths uniting in a mimicry of that sweetness which soon their bodies would share.

Half swooning under the intoxicating taste and feel of him, Sorrel clutched on his shoulders, her lashes fluttering down on to her cheeks as his mouth left hers to trail slow, tormenting fire down her throat. Then his hand cupped one of her breasts, his touch searing her skin through the fragile silk of her dress.

His thumb stroked across the delicate centre and, instantly engorged and throbbing, it thrust against him as, lost to sensations almost terrifying in their intensity, she arched against him with a wild abandonment which, at another time and in another world, would have shamed her. But Matt was drawing from her responses which were transforming her totally, and after tonight she would never again be the same Sorrel Elliot.

Her fingernails raked across his back until, after dragging his shirt from his waistband, she slid her hands beneath the fine poplin to revel in the tautness of his muscles as they flexed under her palms.

She felt his hands go to her zip, then he was sliding down the dress, peeling her out of it. He eased it down over her thighs then, slowly kneeling at her feet, his face intent, the green eyes shadowed by the long black lashes, he drew the flimsy silk down her legs until she could step out of it.

Sitting back on his haunches, he surveyed her slender body, naked now except for the dainty white cotton panties, his eyes openly feasting on every delicate curve — the swell of her breasts, rose-pink in the glow from the wall-lights, the long, lovely line from them to her waist and hips.

'Your skin is perfect,' he said huskily as she stood smiling at him. 'Smooth as silk. And your body — it smells of nectar, like a meadow of summer flowers.'

Putting his hands on her hips, he drew her to him and buried his face in her belly. The sensation was so entirely physical that it was like a knife, thrust through her vitals. Her whole body sagging, she slid to her knees, and together they fell to the floor, the deep carpet cushioning them. And then she was pulling Matt to her, and both of them were trembling with urgency.

The insistent sound of the phone was on the very periphery of her conscious-ness, far beyond Matt's ragged breathing and the wild tumult of her own heart. But then she stiffened.

'Matt — the phone.'

He muttered an incoherent oath. 'Let the damn thing ring. It won't be important.'

'No, no — you must answer it.' Caressing his face with a loving hand, she even managed a teasing smile. 'Surely no call for the great Mateo Ramirez is ever unimportant.' And as he gave a mock scowl she went on softly, 'After all, we have the whole night, haven't we?'

'All right, witch.' He gently tugged a tousled strand of silky hair. 'But, I promise you, you'll pay for this later.' As he pulled away from her he went on shakily, 'Oh, God, I didn't intend it to be like this. I was going to spin it out, golden drop by golden drop, until — ' He was on his feet now, smiling down at her, his eyes very dark, his cheeks flushed.

'Until?' she prompted, as he went across to the phone.

'Oh — until, driven crazy by my superb technique, you were weeping for me to take you. And instead here I am on the carpet, like some steamy adolescent.'

Crooking the receiver with his little finger, he dropped on to the sofa. 'Ramirez here. Oh, hello, Steve . . . Well, you certainly choose your moments.' He slanted a smile at Sorrel. 'Did you leave something behind? I'll check with Jorge . . . No? What is it, then?'

She lay, one arm half shading her eyes, watching him, her gaze tracing every beloved line of that tough, handsome face. He caught her glance and flashed her a smile before returning his attention to the phone, and at that smile something in her tightened unbearably.

He hadn't told her he loved her, of course, and when she'd seen some of the women he mixed with — at the theatre, then at that restaurant last week and, even worse, tonight — she'd been filled with a sense of utter inadequacy. But now, looking at him, she thought with sudden fierceness, Somehow I'll make him love me.

'I see.' Wrapped in her own thoughts, she was barely aware of Matt speaking. 'Yes — yes, Steve, I'm very grateful . . . No, you were quite right to let me know.'

He replaced the receiver and came slowly back, to stand gazing down at her with a strange expression — almost, she thought involuntarily, as though he was committing her upturned face to memory, as if he was never going to see it again.

There was something in his utter stillness which was unnerving, but finally, after a silence which had lasted an aeon of time, he said softly, 'You haven't told me lately — how is that series of yours coming on?'

'Series?' She stared up at him blankly through the veil of tangled hair.

'Don't tell me you've forgotten.' His voice was still soft, sibilant, even, but all at once there was a wholly new quality in him — something jagged, dangerous — that she had never glimpsed before.

' 'The Lifestyles of the World's Wealthiest Men' — that was it, wasn't it? And I was first on your list.'

Sorrel's hands clutched convulsively. 'Oh — that. Well, I — I've put it aside for the moment.'

'Don't lie to me, damn you.'

The sudden ferocity in his voice hit her like a stinging blow across the face. She jerked her head up and met his eyes; an ice-green light was glittering in their pale depths.

'That phone call — ?' she began hesitantly. Her lips were still throbbing from his kisses, so that she could barely speak.

'Precisely. How unfortunate for you that one of your fellow guests tonight came up against your little band of dirt-rakers a couple of months ago. Insider-dealing was what they were trying to pin on him, I gather. The rumours turned out to be totally unfounded and they had to back off, but not before they'd stirred up one hell of a hassle for him.'

'But I wasn't involved in that.' She shook her head, desperate to clear it, but the effects of Matt's passionate lovemaking, and then of this savage verbal assault, had totally disorientated her.

'Maybe not, but just in case Tarre decided to come back for a second go, Steve made it his business to get the personal details of all of you, including photographs. Apparently he's spent the evening puzzling over where he'd seen you before, and it's only just hit him. He called me on his car-phone — thought I should be tipped off, in case I was the next target for the jackal-pack.'

'We are not jackals!' Despite her spiralling fear, Sorrel's eyes flashed. 'OK, sometimes the information proves false, and we drop an investigation. But some things need exposing — the Bryden Tarre column fills a social need.'

His lips tightened. 'Oh, yes, and what particular *social need* are you aiming to fill in exposing me? I presume that this is what the last three weeks have been about?'

No, Matt. The last three weeks have been about me falling desperately, hopelessly in love with you . . .

'If you're so proud of your job,' he continued inexorably, 'there can be just one reason why you lied to me.'

'I didn't lie, Matt.' In her urgency she sat up, then, remembering that she was all but naked, caught up the pink dress and clutched it to her. 'I just didn't tell you everything. I really do have plans to write that series — on a freelance basis.'

'But you somehow forgot to tell me that you're on the payroll of that sleaze-rag — and that can only be because you were trying to get your claws into me. Well?' he demanded harshly as she stayed silent.

'It wasn't like that, Matt. You must believe me.' She gazed up at him imploringly, but his face was basalt-hard, so she went on tremblingly, 'Yes, we were investigating you.'

25

'And just what crime against humanity am I supposed to have committed?'

She took a deep breath, then said flatly, 'We were given information — very convincing information — that you were using your position as head of the Bank of Tierranueva to launder drugs money.'

'Drugs money!' He looked totally stunned.

'It would be so easy for you — a Central American bank, ideally placed on the drugs route to the States and Europe, you free to travel the world. You must see, Matt,' she said, desperate for him at least to understand. 'An accusation like that — we had to follow it up. But — '

'And may I ask who gave you this information?' The silky smoothness of his voice did nothing to hide the white heat of his anger. It seared her skin.

'You know I can't tell you that.' She was looking straight ahead at the opposite wall.

His hands bunched at his sides and,

terrified that he was going to seize hold of her, she flinched away. But then he gave a harsh laugh.

'Of course not. Good journalists never reveal their sources — though they've gone to gaol for it. But don't worry, my sweet. There are other ways of discovering that than shaking it out of a worthless little tramp.'

'Matt — don't,' she said unsteadily, her eyes blurring as a hairline crack ran through her heart.

'Oh, please.' His lips twisted into a sneer. 'We both know what a superb little actress you are, so spare us both the tears.'

'I'm not acting. I — '

'What do you call it, then? You were planted on me, weren't you? To play the whore.'

'No!' She put a trembling hand to her mouth.

'Pillow talk — that was your role in the operation, wasn't it? Well, aren't you going to deny it?' A guilty flush at the echo of Bryden's words suffused her paper-white face. 'Oh, you've been very subtle, I give you that — with those wide, beautiful, oh, so innocent eyes.'

Going down on his haunches, he caught hold of her chin, dragging her face round so that she was forced to look into his chill eyes.

'God, what a fool I've been!' His voice was thick with flaying self-contempt. 'Treating you like a cut-glass virgin.'

'But — '

'Oh, you were patient — nothing so crude as leaping into bed on our first date. So why the sudden change of gear? Couldn't you contain your itch for it any longer? Or are they pushing for results back at Planet House?'

'No, they're not.' She laid a tentative hand on his shirt-sleeve, but he brushed it off as though she were a crawling insect. Forcing down the shaft of pain, she went on, 'In fact, when I report back tomorrow, I'm sure they'll call the whole investigation off. I intend to tell them that you're innocent.'

'And what makes you so sure of that?' His voice was jagged with menace.

'I know you could never do such a thing, because I — ' She broke off, biting her lower lip.

'Well?'

'Because I l-love you.' It was no more than a broken whisper.

'Love me?' He stared at her for a long moment, as if frozen, then gave a shaky laugh. 'You know, *querida*, you really should be on the stage — you almost had me fooled for a moment.' His green eyes were bleak. 'So you really expect this whole operation to be cancelled when you go in tomorrow and lisp, 'I know he's innocent, Bryden, because I l-love him.' '

'Please, Matt — don't!' She flung her hands to her ears, barely conscious that the silk dress had fallen away to expose her naked breasts.

'Or is that the only evidence? Well?' His hands seized on her bare shoulders like talons and he shook her.

'Please, Matt,' she said again, on a little sob of terror. 'I've done nothing — I swear it.'

'I wonder.' He stared down at her, his eyes like green chips of ice. 'You were left alone here for an hour this afternoon. Just how did you pass the time, I wonder?'

And at her guilty flush he sent her sprawling on the carpet as he leapt to his feet. Her hands clutched to her face, she lay listening to his rapid steps cross to the study. The door opened, then moments later he was back, standing over her again.

When she dragged her eyes back to him she saw, with a sickening lurch of her stomach, that he was holding the very computer disk she had taken out earlier.

'I suppose Jorge disturbed you.' His voice chilled her to the marrow. 'You were in such a hurry that you put it back out of order, or I would never have known.'

As her frozen lips moved he went on

harshly, 'Don't bother to deny it — I can see the guilt in your eyes. Like a cheap hacker, you've broken into my personal file. And you could hardly believe your luck, I don't doubt, when you found the dynamite that's in here.'

As he jabbed viciously at the disk Sorrel ran the tip of her tongue round her mouth, but still no words would come.

'Oh, nothing incriminating, nothing dishonest,' he snarled, 'but the information here would be priceless to my competitors. But why am I telling you this? You know it already.'

'No!' At last she was stung into speech. 'You've got it all wrong, Matt. And if you don't believe me — ' his lip had curled in contempt ' — where's the print-out? There's my bag.' She gestured at it wildly. 'Search it — search my clothes.'

'Thank you, but no.' His lips curled in a sneer. 'I wouldn't lower myself — and anyway, no doubt you've been cleverer than that. It's all stored away in that sharp little personal computer of yours that you call a brain.' The fury was vibrating in his voice now. 'And, of course, you weren't planning on wasting this on Tarre, were you? Oh, no, when you saw just what you'd got your greedy little hands on, you were going to sell it to the highest bidder.'

'No! No, I wasn't.' She was dying inside, but still she struggled to convince him. 'And you must see, Matt, if I was so sure of your innocence, that at least shows that I didn't *need* to s-sleep with you.'

'Perhaps not, but you were still hot enough for it just now — and the thought of what you had over me would have added an extra spice to it.' His voice flicked over her raw wounds like a whip. 'Well — maybe I won't disappoint you, after all.'

'No, Matt — no!'

At the expression in his eyes stark terror gripped her, and she tried to scramble to her feet. But her heel caught in a fold of pink silk and as she fell headlong across him his fingers clamped on her arms like talons of steel, biting into the soft flesh.

'L-let me go.' Stark terror was gripping her.

'Not just yet, my darling. I told you — you smell of flowers and honey. Well, I'll bury myself in that sweetness.'

'No! Please, Matt — you can't!'

'Oh, but I can.' His face was a merciless mask. 'Women who use their bodies to get what they want need to be taught a lesson, and by the time tonight is over you'll have learnt it.'

Jack-knifing to his feet, he snatched her up, even as she rolled desperately away, and, holding her in his arms, he strode out through the hallway. He shouldered his bedroom door open, then closed it behind them with a kick and flung her down on the wide bed. As she opened her mouth to cry out he clapped a hand across it.

'Save your screams of outraged virtue. Those girls have gone, and Jorge is too well-trained to interfere. And anyway, it's what you want, isn't it?'

Straightening up, he began to strip off his clothes with an intensity which so terrified her that every muscle locked, and she lay, quite unable even to try and escape.

When he came down beside her she gave one faint whimper, but he smothered it, taking it into his hot mouth. This was the other side of his supreme physicality — the power, the sheer sexual drive, which he had kept fiercely reined in. Now, though, he was deliberately unleashing it.

As he moved across her, forcing her thighs apart to admit him, she twisted her head away, but, catching her by the jaw, he wrenched her face round to him.

'No, damn you. I want to see your expression when I take you.'

Tears were burning behind her eyes but she wouldn't cry — she'd deny him that pleasure, at least. But when she felt him tense, to thrust hard against her tender flesh, she bit her inner lip, and the salty taste of blood filled her mouth as she steeled herself for the ultimate violation.

But then, in that final second, he was pushing her away, so violently that she rolled to the very edge of the bed. Utterly bewildered, she lay, intense spasms racking her slender body. One arm was thrown up across her face, and her hair was tangled where his fingers had raked through it. Hardly conscious, she felt the bed sag for an instant, and when she opened her eyes he was on the other side of the room, dressing.

'Sorry to disappoint you after all.' The voice was barely recognisable. 'I've never slept with a whore yet, and I'm not starting with you.'

He turned towards the door.

'Wh — where are you going?' she whispered.

'Out — for a long drive.' Still he did not look at her.

'No — no, Matt.' Her love for him overwhelmed everything else and she struggled up on to one elbow. 'Don't drive — not in this mood.'

He gave a faint shrug, and for a moment she thought he was going without another word, but then he came back to the bed and looked down at her, his eyes bleak.

'I want you gone — out of my house, out of my life — when I get back. You'll excuse me if I don't take you home. I'll call you a cab.'

'There's no need,' she replied, with a pathetic touch of pride, but he was already taking up the bedside phone and punching out a number.

He spoke briefly, then set it down. 'He'll be here in ten minutes. Let yourself out. Oh, and just one more thing.' He turned slowly to look at her. 'The contents of that disk are known only to one person beside myself, so if there should be a leak I shall know who is responsible. Do I make myself clear?'

The unspoken threat hung in the air and she nodded, barely perceptibly.

'Good. I'm glad we understand each other.'

Picking up his car keys from the dressing-table, he dropped them into his pocket and turned away. But then, his hand still in his pocket, he stopped dead. Drawing something out, he looked down at it, a strange expression on his face, then tossed it on to the bed beside her. It was a small cream leather box.

'I got this for you this afternoon — ' his lips twisted ' — while you were otherwise occupied. You may as well have it. I wouldn't insult any other woman by giving it to her. Open it.'

'No.' She shrank away from the tiny box. 'No, I don't want to.'

'Open it, damn you.'

At the raw savagery in his voice she snatched it up and fumbled with the catch. Inside, cradled on white silk, was a superb dark sapphire and diamond ring. She looked from it to Matt; his face, pale under his tan, was expressionless.

'Yes, that's right. It's an engagement ring. Tonight, my sweet, as you lay in my arms in this bed, I was going to ask you to marry me.' His voice was flat, empty of all emotion. 'You see, Sorrel, I thought I was in love with you.'

I thought I was in love with you. The words were like a knell, as a dreadful, desolate feeling of loss swept through her.

'Please, Matt — '

'Now what do you want?'

She wanted him to take her in his arms, hold her, and then everything would still be all right, but she could only gaze up at him in mute appeal.

'Don't look at me like that, with those damn witch's eyes. It won't work, I tell you — I know you too well for that.'

He was breaking her heart, shattering it into tiny bleeding fragments. She looked down at the ring, the beautiful stones shimmering and blurring, for just one final, wrenching moment, then she snapped the box shut and held it out to him, her hand almost steady.

'Take it, Matt. I don't want it.'

'As you wish.'

Very carefully, so that his fingers did not come into contact with hers, he took the little box, then slid open the heavy plate glass window and hurled it out into the darkness for the river to take. Next moment he had gone, leaving her to lie, a huddled heap, her knees drawn up, rocking slightly to and fro in silent misery.

Only her pride finally forced her to her feet. She crossed to the open window, and automatically she closed it. The rain was still trickling down the pane. It really is like tears, she thought.

All at once her stiff features began to crumple, but then, through her desolation, she vowed, I will not cry. Not now, not ever for Matt Ramirez.

2

Bliss!

Sorrel gave another long, languorous stretch of her silky limbs then very slowly sat up, propping herself against the scratchy trunk of the palm tree.

Below the jutting headland, that perfect bay was still deserted, its long sweeping crescent of pale cream sand empty of footprints, the milky green translucent water rippling undisturbed on to the beach. The only sounds — since that helicopter, which had dropped down to land unseen in the grounds of the villa, all but invisible in its thick greenery on the opposite headland — were the faint whisper of the waves and the dry rustle of palm fronds overhead.

Ben hadn't exaggerated — it really was paradise here. Maybe she'd stay forever, never go back to London.

She'd become a Barbados beach bum. Her lips tugged in a wry smile. Just because you've been ill, that's no reason to become self-indulgent at the ripe old age of twenty-four, Sorrel, my girl, she told herself sternly. Get down there, make Man Friday tracks through that creamy talcum powder, and have a long, lazy swim.

She'd been right to stay up here, sheltered by this tree — it was only the second full day of her holiday and there wasn't an iota of shade down there. But the searing afternoon heat was fading now, so she got to her feet, brushing some tiny dead leaves off her wet-look pink bikini.

First, though, she must take a photograph, before the sun sank any lower. Pity she couldn't be in it, with someone else taking it . . . Then that someone would come down to join her, and hand in hand they'd splash out into the waves, happy and laughing . . .

'*Stop it*!' she said aloud, fiercely. She *was* happy — far, far happier this way.

41

She lifted the camera, but then lowered it abruptly as through the viewfinder she saw half a dozen men appear from among the tangle of shrubs and trees at the far end of the beach. The tiny figures were making for a wooden jetty, and at the same instant a white launch appeared, cutting swiftly through the water towards them.

As the first man reached the jetty he glanced round sharply. From across the curving half-moon of beach he saw her, and it seemed to Sorrel as if, for long seconds, their gazes locked. But then he beckoned urgently to two of the other men, and then he was pointing in her direction — pointing directly at her, for all the heads swivelled. Next moment, the two men jumped down on to the sand and began heading purposefully towards her.

Oh, no! Sorrel let out a groan. This must be one of the private beaches on the island — no wonder it was deserted at the height of the tourist season! She must be trespassing, and those two men in khaki shirts and shorts — they were near enough now for her to see — were no doubt coming to tell her so, in no uncertain terms. They'd frog-march her back to the track — or, even worse, drag her down to the irate owner to grovel her apologies.

There were no 'Private' signs up here, though, so she could stand her ground and argue it out. Any other time she would have done, but today she really didn't feel up to any angry confrontations. So, slipping back among the hibiscus bushes, she snatched up her beach towel, crammed her book, suntan oil, floppy hat and camera into the big straw bag she had bought that morning in the craft market in Bridgetown, and fled.

At the big white gates leading into the complex where she was staying she paused to snatch a hurried glance over her shoulder. Good — the men weren't in sight. They probably thought she'd taken the other track, back to the point where tourists often parked their mini mokes.

She relaxed, eased her flurried breathing and, doing her best to look nonchalant, strolled through the attractively landscaped grounds to the groundfloor apartment which Ben had loaned her.

'You've been driving yourself too hard,' he'd told her severely, after yet again she'd almost passed out at a meeting with a client. 'For heaven's sake, take a break, Sorrel, or you'll be no good to either of us. I've just had a cancelled booking on my apartment out in Barbados, so go home and pack your bikini and your suntan oil — and no arguments.'

Inside she found the maid, running a mop over the tiled floor.

'Evening, Miss Elliot.' Her cheerful face creased in a broad smile.

'Hello, Victoria.' Sorrel returned the smile warmly.

'You still looking peaky, miss — real peaky.' The woman scrutinised her until she shifted uncomfortably.

'Oh, no — I'm feeling much better already.'

'Well, you go and have yourself a shower, then I'll bring you a cold drink on the patio.'

'Yes, all right.'

Sorrel gave in meekly, and went through to her air-conditioned bedroom. Ben had warned her about Victoria — the number one bossy-boots on the island, he'd said. But really it was quite nice being fussed over — just once in a while, of course.

It suddenly seemed a very long time since anyone had pampered her. And whose fault's that? a sneaky little voice whispered as she stripped off her swimsuit and went through to the shower. Maybe it's because you've never allowed them to . . .

It was very quiet out on her small patio, with its white criss-cross of trellis covered with tumbling pink and mauve bougainvillaea — so quiet that she could hear the ice cubes in her lime juice tinkling softly each time she took a sip from the tall glass. Too quiet. For all at once into her mind — as always when there was nothing to distract her — came the image, five years old, of Matt Ramirez.

She'd seen him several times since. Oh, not in the flesh, of course, but occasionally his photograph would appear in the business pages when his bank was involved in yet another complex financial deal. Then, once, she'd been under the dryer at the hairdresser's when the assistant had smilingly set a pile of glossy magazines on her knee, and she'd found herself staring down at him.

His arm had been round the stunning brunette who that year had come very close to winning Miss World — or some such title — for his own Central American state. The girl had been gazing up at him with undisguised rapture, while he had looked . . . But who had ever known what Matt Ramirez was thinking? Sorrel had thought savagely. Who could hope to guess at what was going on behind those opaque, enigmatic eyes?

And then, in her flat one evening, she'd switched on the television — and there he'd been, engrossed in a round-the-table discussion on the eve of what she'd gathered was a crucial meeting of the International Monetary Fund.

With trembling hands she'd slotted a video cassette in place, then had sat, as though held in a giant, crushing fist, listening to that velvet-harsh voice, watching every slight nuance of expression on his face — that cynical tilt of the mouth, the pale green eyes like a watchful cat's, the very slight, irritable tapping of one of those long tanned fingers which, perhaps unnoticed by any other viewer, had told her that his incisive mind was only just coping with the less acute intellects around him.

She'd watched that tiny piece of video — sandwiched between two favourite Fred Astaire movies — over and over, with a kind of ferocious, gnawing hunger which could never be appeased. And then, quite suddenly, one night she'd played it through then gone down on her knees in front of the screen and wiped it — all of it, the entire tape — so that not a vestige should be left . . .

Abruptly Sorrel picked up her glass, drained her drink, then stood up, snapping the fragile thread of her thoughts. She'd have a swim before dinner — she'd only swum once today, so she wouldn't be overdoing it.

In her pink bikini and matching beach wrap, she slipped quietly into the pool area, floodlit now in the warm tropical dusk, and heard shouts and laughter. Those three young Englishmen from the apartment just across the lawn — one of them had been very pressing for her to spend this evening with him at one of the down-town night-spots. He had been very pleasant, and she hadn't really enjoyed refusing him, but . . .

She stood irresolutely, tapping her

foot, then slipped unseen past the pool, across the manicured lawns and on to the beach, still lit by an apricot sunset. It was deserted, like that other beach had been earlier. Last night there had been a barbecue down here, with a steel band and limbo dancers, supple as elastic bands. It had been noisy and fun, and she'd sat with two very friendly Canadian girls from Prince Edward Island, but as the trio of young men had moved in she'd been glad to plead convalescence and slip away.

Now there was only her. Shedding her beach wrap on the warm sand, she waded out into the water, cool as silk against her clammy body, and struck out. After a while she turned on to her back, and as her hair drifted around her like pale fronds of seaweed she relaxed her limbs, letting the water take her, rock her gently to and fro. Above her head was the new moon, a pale sliver, and a million diamond points of stars . . .

A fish, smooth as satin, brushed her

leg then twisted away, its tail flicking against her thigh. She jumped slightly, then, as she rolled on to her front, gave a little gasp. The lights of the apartments were tiny pinpricks, the circle of lamps around the pool and dining-area just a pale blur. Gently lulled by the sea, she had drifted a long way — a very long way — from the shore.

Kicking herself round in the water, she began swimming towards the land, but realised two things in the same instant. One — the wind had got up, so that the waves were splashing in her face, and two — she was quite suddenly very tired. Blind panic surged through her; she'd never make it — she'd drown, alone, out here.

Looking round in desperation, she saw that she was nearer to a line of rocks with a rugged headland above them, black against the last scarlet streaks of sunset. Keeping her eyes on that dark bulk she swam towards it, driving herself through the water until her breath was rasping in her lungs. She was moving more and more slowly, though, her legs not flesh and muscle but leaden weights to be forced through liquid concrete.

A wave struck her sideways on, then another, rippling along behind it, so that she gulped in seawater, the salt stinging her throat and eyes. She blinked, squeezed them shut, then opened them again and saw, just ahead of her, a line of lights.

She was hallucinating — light-headed from sheer, mind-numbing exhaustion. But she drove herself on, every stroke an agony of effort, until it would almost have been easier — much easier — to let go, surrender to the sea . . . Grimly, she gritted her teeth and battled on . . .

Her fingers brushed against hard metal, and, focusing her blurred eyes, she realised with an overwhelming lift of the heart that she had swum right into a yacht — a large one, with a smooth white hull which towered over her.

She scrabbled for purchase but slipped back, and when she tried to call for help only a choked croak emerged. She was going to drown, right here, beside this boat. Then, as weak tears filled her eyes, her despairing fingers closed on a rope, and just beside her was a flight of narrow steps.

Sobbing for breath, she all but, lacked the strength to haul herself up them, and once at the top she collapsed on to the glossy varnished deck on all fours, her head hanging as she fought to get the life back into her lungs.

When finally she raised her eyes she saw lights coming from the cabin area and tottered across the deck, her legs as wobbly as a baby taking its first staggering steps. What would she say? 'Hi, I'm a mermaid — just dropped in.' Something like that. She bit her lip as a weak giggle bubbled up inside her. Then they'd give her a hot shower, something to drink, maybe, and she'd be back at her apartment in time for dinner — before anyone had missed her.

She raised her hand to knock on the window, but then let it rest in mid-air, her muscles all at once frozen. There were several men inside, just inches away on the other side of the glass, and one of them . . . Sorrel gave a faint gasp. Surely — surely she couldn't be mistaken. That shock of silver-grey hair, the hook nose and dark skin which showed the Amerindian blood. It was Juan del Castillo, head of one of Latin America's biggest industrial conglomerates, though Sorrel, along with half the Western world, knew him more for his juicy play-boy lifestyle.

Her hand hung in space a moment longer, but as she took a backward step away from the saloon window she cannoned into a hard body. Two pairs of arms went round her, crushing her, and a hand gripped her mouth, silencing every fragment of the cry of terror which had surged up in her.

But the terror gave her strength. She

fought like a wild thing against those steel arms, biting the hand so that, with an oath in a language she did not understand, it was withdrawn. Even as she sucked in her breath, though, the hand was replaced by another, the fingers digging viciously into her soft mouth so that, with no apparent effort on the men's part, she was half carried, half dragged along the deck and into a dimly lit passageway.

Outside a door she was pinned against the wall, one man's arm clamped hard across her chest, while her other captor knocked softly, almost tentatively.

'*Entre!*'

Above her rasping breath, Sorrel scarcely heard the word of command, but the man opened the door and went in. There were a few brief words from him, then another voice — barely audible, but curt, authoritative.

The man reappeared, his face tinged a dusky red — and not only, she guessed, from where her flailing fist had caught it. He seized her left arm, bringing it up behind her until tears of pain sprang to her eyes, then both men pushed her inside ahead of them.

After the dark passage, the cabin was too bright for her sore eyes. She winced, blinking in the light which reflected off the gleaming mahogany panelling, then gradually focused on a man, his back to them, seated at a leather-topped desk. He was writing, and went on writing until they came up just behind him, though he must have heard them, in spite of the dense-pile white carpet.

'*Señor.*'

One of her guards spoke, and Sorrel saw the man lay down a gold fountain pen, then very deliberately swivel round in his chair. And finally — as behind the screen of wet, tangled hair her eyes dilated with shock, very slowly at first, then more quickly — she folded up at the feet of Matt Ramirez.

★ ★ ★

All she could see was the pattern of the sofa — a William Morris design, she registered inconsequentially — on which someone had laid her. Fearfully, barely breathing, she turned her head and saw, through the strands of hair which plastered her face, that the two men had gone. She was alone in the cabin now — except for Matt, who was standing propped against the desk, his tanned arms folded across his black T-shirt, his pale green eyes regarding her. And at the expression in them her stomach performed a quick flip-dive of fear.

She tried to struggle to her feet, but as a fresh wave of dizziness took her, threatening to overwhelm her again, she collapsed back against the cushions.

Levering himself upright, he came across to stand looking down at her, his thumbs stuck in the leather belt of his white canvas jeans. As he surveyed her his mouth twisted slightly and, glancing down, she realised with a strangled gasp that in the struggle her pink bikini top had been wrenched down, so that her full breasts were all but exposed to his cold eyes.

He watched with clinical impassivity as she tugged it back up, her cheeks blazing with colour.

'Get up.'

Sorrel winced at the chill hostility in his voice. Oh, she could hardly have expected a 'How lovely to see you again, *querida*', but surely five years on he should have forgiven her — as she had forgiven him. But men like Ramirez never did forgive, did they? To them, something so human would be a sign of weakness.

'I said, get up,' he repeated harshly.

'I really don't think I should,' she replied, in as cool a tone as she could muster. 'I'll probably pass out again if I do. Could I have a drink of water, please — that's if it's not too much trouble for you?' she added, grateful for the touch of waspishness in her voice.

His lips tightened, but then he went over to a washbasin in the corner, filled a glass and held it out to her. Very cautiously, she raised herself against the cushions and took a few sips.

Over the tilted rim of the glass, she surreptitiously regarded Matt. Older — more than five years older, somehow . . . A few grey hairs in that thick black thatch, a deep perpendicular cleft between his dark brows, the face taut, the mouth set in a grim line which seemed habitual . . . And yet even more handsome — the vicious stab of pain took her quite by surprise. But the cruelty which had lurked in those beautiful black-fringed eyes was still there . . . Though maybe that was only when he looked in her direction.

'Thanks.' She handed the glass back to him and he set it down on the desk.

Picking up a chair, he swung it round and sat astride it, his chin propped on his hand, those chill, inimical eyes on her. They revealed nothing, yet behind them she sensed his razor mind at work, and that only increased her growing sense of unease.

'Thank goodness your boat was here,'

she said, with an attempt at a rueful smile. 'It is your boat, isn't it?' A slight nod. 'Out there in the darkness, I really thought I was going to — ' Her voice shook, and she bit her lip as wisps of that terror stirred in her again. 'When I saw the boat, I thought it was a mirage, but — '

'You have lost none of your old talent, I see.' That voice — its icy antagonism — froze her. Yet once it had murmured such sweet endearments . . . *No.* Don't remember, she told herself fiercely.

'Old talent?' She looked at him blankly. 'I don't know what you mean, Matt.'

'Oh, come now, my dear, we both know what a consummate actress you are. Those sapphire eyes, as wide and appealing as ever.' Reaching across, he caught hold of her face, wrenching it up to the light. 'Yes, my crew — poor, defenceless males that they are — would have swallowed every line of every lie you spun them.'

'No! It's not a lie.'

'How it must have upset your devious plans to come face to face with me. No wonder you passed out.'

Sorrel opened her mouth in angry denial, but then expelled a long breath. It doesn't matter what this swine thinks of you — just keep telling yourself that. What matters is that you get the hell out of here — away from him — as far away as you can.

Experimentally she swung her legs to the floor and sat forward, but Matt pushed her back into the sofa.

'Stay right there.' It was very softly spoken, but she obeyed. 'You were discovered, your greedy face all but pressed to the glass of the saloon in your eagerness to hear what — '

'Look,' she broke in, 'if you choose to entertain a man like that — Oh, but of course.' Her befuddled mind cleared slightly. 'He's from Tierranueva, isn't he? And maybe you're birds of a feather, you and del Castillo.'

'So you did recognise him.' His voice

fell even lower, but there was something in it which made the tiny blonde hairs on her nape stand on end.

'Recognise del Castillo?' She gave an incredulous laugh. 'Of course I did. You don't get to be one of the world's great playboys for twenty years without becoming *fairly* well-known. And I was a journalist — '

'Was?' he queried sharply.

'Yes. I — I've left the Bryden Tarre team.' Unable to meet his eyes, she picked at a thread in the sofa cushion.

'Really?' He raised one sardonic brow.

'Yes — I decided it wasn't my scene.' Nothing would get out of her the admission that in reality, the morning following that last terrible encounter in his flat, she'd gone into Planet House and handed in her notice.

No need, either, to recall the bitter irony that on that very same day the reports had come in from Tierranueva confirming Matt's innocence and saying that the evidence against him had been concocted by a former employee who'd been dismissed for embezzlement. So she needn't have even contemplated breaking into his computer after all . . .

'So, how do you earn your living now?'

She wouldn't allow the undisguised sneer in his tone to get to her. 'I write computer programs,' she said flatly.

'Oh, but of course. I'd quite forgotten that manipulation of computer keyboards is another of your many — talents.'

'Let's just drop this, shall we?' Her voice was brittle as glass. Surely he must see that she simply wasn't up to this verbal sparring — although when had that ever stopped Matt Ramirez from moving in for the kill? she thought bitterly.

'But you've no doubt kept up your journalistic contacts?'

'I've still got friends in the business, yes. But what's that to you?'

'And you've lost none of your nose for a story — especially where there is money in it for you.'

In the heat of the cabin, it seemed as though a freezer door had been flung open in her face. But five years on she would not let him see how much his words hurt her.

She shrugged. 'If you say so, Matt.'

'It was you out on that headland this afternoon, wasn't it?'

'This afternoon? You mean — you were one of those men?'

So Matt had been there, among those faraway figures. And even at that distance some invisible thread had seemed to tug between them . . .

'You saw del Castillo — and he obviously didn't want to be seen — so you decided it just might be worth sussing out what he was up to, no matter what damage you might do in the process.'

'Oh, how ridiculous,' Sorrel exploded. 'All right — he's here on board, and he's a fellow countryman of yours. But I don't see how it can 'damage' your precious reputation to be seen consorting with him. I suppose you've turned your yacht into some kind of private love-nest for him and his friends. But if that's your idea of doing somebody a favour, well,' she hurtled on recklessly, 'that's up to — '

'Be quiet!'

His voice slashed through her words like a chainsaw, and as she sat back abruptly she saw that beneath his suntan there was a dangerous line of colour along his cheekbones.

'Do not provoke me, Sorrel, or — ' He broke off, obviously fighting for self-control.

'Or, what? Or you'll complete what you almost did last time we met. Is that what you're threatening me with, Matt — rape?'

The ugly monosyllable hung in the air between them like a fizzing stick of dynamite. For long seconds they stared into one another's eyes, but then his thin lips twisted.

'Don't be alarmed, *querida*. I would

not lower myself to lay one finger on you.'

The contempt in his voice was flaying her, but she would not let him see it. He might have broken her heart five years ago, but that Sorrel Elliot had been different — soft, vulnerable. The new Sorrel was a far more formidable opponent — as he'd find out.

'I'm so glad,' she said coldly. 'Your lovemaking technique, such as it was — ' His brows came down in a black frown, but she would not be silenced. 'Such as it was,' she repeated, 'left much to be desired. And I don't imagine it has improved any.'

She saw his hands tighten on the chair-back, but even as she shrank away from him, terrified at what she might have unleashed, there was a discreet knock at the cabin door.

'*Entre!*' Matt snapped, his eyes still trained on her, and a young man — one she had not seen before — in a white uniform came in.

He closed the door, shot one quick glance in her direction, then turned all his attention to Matt, who was giving what sounded like a series of rapid orders. The young man nodded deferentially, then went out, silently closing the door behind him.

Matt stood up and sauntered across to her — as predatory, as panther-like as ever, she thought involuntarily — and dropped on to the sofa, his thigh against hers, just the white canvas of his jeans between them. That thigh felt intensely warm, intensely alive — intensely masculine. Every nerve-ending in her leg began to tingle, as if a sharp burst of electric current had run through it, and she edged furtively away from him.

'I have ordered some coffee for you.' His gaze swept over her critically. 'You look as though you could do with some — in fact, you look quite appalling.'

Without warning, he lifted his hand to pluck a wet strand of hair from her cheek and tuck it behind her ear. The tiny gesture set the electricity flowing again — this time a prickling sensation where his fingertips had brushed her cheek.

She stared at him, her eyes blank, then somehow pulled herself together. 'Well, thanks very much. If you'd been half drowned out there tonight, you wouldn't be looking your best, either.' She essayed a pale ghost of a smile, but he did not respond. 'But in any case, I haven't been well — I've been overdoing things at work, and Ben said — '

'Ben?' he interposed sharply.

'My partner — my *business* partner,' she amended, although there wasn't the slightest reason why she had to make that distinction clear to him. 'We run a company together, constructing computer programs to firms' individual requirements.'

'And your business is flourishing, I hope.'

'We're doing well enough,' she replied woodenly.

'Well enough, certainly, to afford a luxury vacation in Barbados. Unless, of course, you are still augmenting your income from other — sources.'

'Actually — ' Sorrel clamped her teeth on the hurt ' — the apartment belongs to Ben. He's loaned it to me for a couple of weeks. And, talking of Halcyon Beach, I'd better be getting back there — or they'll be putting out search-parties for me.'

She spoke lightly enough, but inside, all at once, she felt herself filled with a desperate need to be safely away from Matt — away from his hostility, his sneering contempt. But more, much more, away from his physical allure which, in spite of everything, was insidiously weaving itself around her — the feel of him as his leg carelessly brushed hers, making all the little golden hairs on her calf stir, the scent of his aftershave, that warm, spicy tang which she remembered so well, and, just beneath that, the aroma — musky and more elusive — that was Matt.

Her skin was clammy, and her heart was pounding suddenly, so that she half rose to her feet. But then there was another tap at the door and the young man came back in. Without a glance at her, he set down a silver coffee-tray at Matt's elbow, then withdrew.

Matt picked up the brown and cream pottery jug. 'White — no sugar?'

'You remember?' she whispered huskily.

He lifted one shoulder in a casual half-shrug. 'I have a good memory — a very good one, where you are concerned.'

As she bit her lip he handed her the mug. 'A cookie?'

'No, thank you. It'll spoil my dinner.'

Another tentative smile, but still no response, so she buried her nose in her mug. The coffee was strong and aromatic, and she drank greedily. He, though, was cradling his mug in his hands, one long finger tracing round the rim as he stared down into the swirling liquid.

'Mmm, that's better,' she said, as its warmth spread through her chilled limbs, 'but I'm afraid I still don't feel up to swimming all the way back to the shore. Do you think you could possibly — ?'

'A boat has been ordered,' he cut in brusquely.

'Oh, thank you. So — you're really letting me go.'

Gladness warred with pain: gladness that he believed her, pain that he should so lightly send her away forever. 'I thought I was in love with you . . . ' 'I thought I was in love with you . . . ' All at once, the five-year-old words were whirling in her mind, until she had to put her hand up to her head, pressing her fingers against her temples. She was beginning to feel very dizzy again.

Her coffee-mug was very heavy. Dimly she was aware of Matt leaping to his feet then taking it from her limp fingers as it began to tilt towards the floor. Someone had filled her legs, her whole body with sawdust, but with a tremendous effort she raised herself to her feet.

'I'm ready,' she tried to say, but the link between her brain and her mouth was broken. She took a couple of stumbling paces towards the swaying cabin door, then as he put his hand on her arm everything — the desk, the tray, Matt's face — spun round her, and went on spinning as she fell into a vortex of darkness.

3

The usual bird was singing its raucous song in the frangipani tree just outside her window. Sorrel stirred, murmured sleepily, then her heavy eyelids fluttered open. Still wrapped in drowsy languor, she rolled over, stretched, then went very still.

This wasn't her room. Oh, the sunlight was streaming in through white louvres, that grackle bird was still squawking outside — but everything else was totally unfamiliar. The light bamboo furniture, the cool turquoise of the curtains and bedspread, had changed in the night to pale bleached wood and warm, earthy tones.

Still blurred with sleep, she slowly sat up, then, as she glanced down at herself, gave a stifled gasp of shock. Instead of her pretty pink cotton nightie she was naked, and round one slim wrist was a ring of bruises. As she stared down at those puffy, bluish-green stains on her skin memory came flooding back.

She saw herself painfully climbing that swaying stairway . . . felt herself seized . . . brutally dragged below . . . saw Matt. At the thought of his cold anger her face screwed up with pain, but then, pushing back the coverlet, she swung her legs to the ground.

But why wasn't she in her own apartment? Had he had her brought to the hotel section of the complex instead? Why hadn't she roused when someone had carried her in here? And — most important of all — she was quite certain that it was not the maid who had undressed her and placed her in this strange bed . . .

Her mouth was as parched as a kiln so, with trembling hands, she poured herself a glass of water from the carafe by the bed and gulped it down. Setting down the glass with a clatter, she got to her feet, dragged the sheet off the bed, wrapped herself in it, then quietly opened the door.

The bedroom led into a large sitting-room, furnished in the same russet and cream tones. There was another green-meshed door at the far end and she pushed it open. But then she halted, one hand leaping to her throat.

She wasn't in the hotel block. There were no immaculate flowerbeds, no curving turquoise pool or bar area with its thatched parasols. Instead, clumps of sprawling mauve oleanders bordered a patch of roughly cut grass, while alongside the house was a simple veranda at the far end of which, sitting at a small pine table, was Matt.

His back was to her and, engrossed in a sheaf of papers laid out in front of him, he had not heard her bare feet on the wooden boards. He was dressed just in an old pair of denim cut-offs; as she watched a muscle tensed beneath the brown satin of his right shoulder when he reached forward to turn over one of the papers, and Sorrel felt her lungs contract hard, painfully, as if they were being crushed.

A faint breathy sigh must have escaped her, for his head suddenly jerked round. For an instant he went very still, openly taking in the slender lines of her body beneath the cotton sheet, and the tangled strands of hair on her shoulders, then he pushed back the chair and came to his feet, crossing the veranda to her.

'Good morning. Or rather — ' he glanced at the slim gold watch at his wrist ' — good afternoon.'

'Afternoon?' Sorrel's jaw dropped. 'How long have I been asleep?'

'Oh, about sixteen hours, give or take the odd minute.'

'Sixteen hours?' she all but shrieked.

'That's what I said.'

'That coffee.' Outrage cleared the last wisps of muzziness from her brain. 'It — it was drugged.'

A danger signal flared along his hard-planed cheekbones. 'I would be very careful before you start hurling more accusations like that.' His voice was clipped, but she ignored the warning in it.

'Yes, it was. How else would I have been out for so long? You — you swine. I might have guessed you'd do something like that.'

'You were not drugged.' He was keeping his voice level with an obvious effort. 'You merely passed out again. To judge from your appearance — ' dispassionately his eyes raked over her pale, taut features ' — you were at least telling the truth about your recent ill-health, so your fatigue did the rest.'

'And who — ?'

'Put you to bed?' he enquired smoothly. 'I did, of course.'

'I see,' she said slowly. But then, furious with herself as she felt the treacherous blush seeping into her face and chest, she went on, 'Well, I'll change back into my bikini right now and then I'm going to walk straight out of here. And you needn't think — '

'Ah, your bikini,' he cut in suavely.

'What about it?' Her voice bristled with suspicion.

'I am sorry, but since I undressed you — ' their eyes met, his green ones bland, hers sparkling sapphires ' — it seems to have been — er — mislaid.'

Their eyes locked again, a long, measuring gaze, then Sorrel put her head in the air, her jaw jutting haughtily.

'Well, in that case, I'll just have to make do with this, won't I?'

Hitching up the folds of white cotton, she took a step away from him, tensing herself to break the world record for the hundred-metres sprint dressed only in a sheet if he tried to grab her. But he did nothing — just leaned in the doorway, arms folded, watching her.

Beyond the oleanders was a wide belt of bamboo, and beyond that again she glimpsed the sparkling aquamarine Caribbean. All the time expecting a heavy hand on her shoulder, she plunged through the bamboo and, feeling slightly foolish, set off resolutely along a beach of powdery white sand which curved away from her to disappear round a headland.

It wound on and on, sometimes petering out so that she was forced to scramble over rough scrub or rocky promontories, and once she had to paddle across a stream, its cool, limpid water tumbling over boulders on to the beach and on into the sea. But she met no one — no swimmers, no sunbathers, no fellow tourists in glass-bottom boats — and when she rounded yet another bend she knew for certain what she'd been suspecting for the last twenty minutes.

The low, white-board house, with its green shutters and its veranda shaded with trailing, blue-starred morning glory and coralita vines, was just as she had left it. And Matt was still lounging in the doorway, watching her as she limped across the rough lawn towards him.

'All right, you've had your little joke.'

Her voice was shaking with temper. 'So — where are we?'

'Not, I'm afraid, on Barbados.'

'I did just gather that,' she said tightly.

'We are on a cay a few miles off the coast. And, in case you have visions of a knight in shining armour arriving to rescue you, I should warn you that it is a private cay. Very private.'

She stared at him, aghast. 'You mean . . . you own it?'

'That's right. I have my villa on Barbados, of course, but — ' he grimaced ' — I need a bolt-hole away from all pressures, where I can relax.'

Did a man like Matt Ramirez ever wholly relax? She doubted it very much.

'But — why have you brought me here?'

'You did not really expect me to swallow that pitiful little story of yours last night, did you?'

Sorrel's hands clenched at her sides, but she merely said, her voice flat, 'It was the truth.' As he looked down at her with a sneer of undisguised disbelief she went on stubbornly, 'But I'll have been missed. Back at the apartments — they'll be worried about me. They'll come looking for me.'

'Oh, no.' He shook his head regretfully. 'A message was sent to Halcyon Beach that you would be dining out and would be away all night. That should not have occasioned any surprise. After all, it will not be the first time that a woman such as you — ' his lip curled ' — chooses to spend a night out of her own bed.'

The vicious knife-thrust of pain was tearing something of the old, vulnerable Sorrel which still lingered. But she would not let him see how much he could still wound her, five long years on. She'd die first.

'Of course not,' she said woodenly. 'But I still don't see why I'm here.'

'Don't you?' He eyed her sardonically. 'I am prepared to accept that you followed del Castillo out to my yacht merely to pick up some juicy titbit to sell to the gossip-rags.'

'No! I — '

'But instead you stumbled on something potentially far more lucrative.'

'What on earth are you talking about?' Sorrel gazed at him blankly.

'Oh, those wide, so-innocent sapphire eyes again.' His mocking tone was like acid. 'Del Castillo was not the only man you saw on my yacht last night, was he?'

She looked at him, puzzled. 'Of course not. There were those two thugs who manhandled me, and then the one who brought the coffee.'

'And?'

She shrugged. 'I was out for the count soon after that — or have you forgotten?'

'So you did not see Ricardo Laborde?'

'I'm sorry,' she replied stiffly, 'I've never heard of him.'

'It is true that he does not figure quite so often in the glossy magazines, but I have no doubt that with your

— investigative talents, you were confident that you would soon get to the truth.'

'The truth?' She shook her head in bewilderment. 'What do you mean?'

He gave her a long, considering look. 'Your agile mind must be well on the way to it by now, but — now that you have been rendered harmless — '

Harmless? What on earth was he talking about? She glanced sharply at him, but his impassive face gave nothing away.

'There is no danger in telling you the rest, if only to show you the story that you are missing.' He paused. 'Laborde and del Castillo are my country's two biggest industrialists by far — between them they own nearly all its manufacturing capacity. For years they have been at daggers drawn, each in turn launching take-over bids against the other. They've managed to fight each other off, but now harsh economic necessity has brought them together. Both companies are in serious trouble, and their only hope is a merger. But if news of such a crisis leaks out prematurely they could both go to the wall.'

'So they're meeting on your yacht?'

He nodded grimly. 'Precisely. Cruising the Caribbean, well away from any inquisitive eyes — or so we thought.'

'But shouldn't you be with them,' she went on hopefully, 'trying to keep the talks going?'

He shook his head. 'I've set up their meeting, but it is down to the two of them now. So, sorry to disappoint you, *querida*, but my best contribution is to stay right here with you. If the talks remain secret for long enough then they just might hammer out an agreement. If, on the other hand, they fail, then my country's already fragile economy will be wrecked. And — ' his eyes narrowed to slivers of tungsten steel ' — I do not intend that to happen merely to satisfy the greed of one mercenary little bitch.'

Another stab of anguish drove into her, so that she almost felt herself bleeding inside.

'But I wouldn't dream of ruining your country — you must believe me, Matt,' she said unsteadily.

'Must I?' He met her imploring gaze with chill indifference. 'Since when did moral scruples stand in the way of a fast buck, as far as you're concerned? I found that out five years ago, and I've no reason to think you've changed.'

Shoulders sagging wearily, she lapsed into silence. What was the good? Until his dying day he would choose to think the worst of her, and the sooner she accepted that, the better.

'But I still don't see — how could I hope to make money out of information like this?'

'Their rival companies throughout Latin America are already circling like jackals. Any one of them would pay very highly for advance information on these merger talks.'

'So you'll be keeping me here until

they're settled, one way or the other?'

'Of course.'

'But that could be days — weeks, even. I'm due back in London in just over a week.'

He shrugged. 'That's your problem.'

'Well, what about Halcyon Beach, then? If I don't turn up today, they really will think something's wrong.'

Without replying, he walked past her to the table and ripped a clean sheet of paper from a pad.

'Come and sit down.'

What was in his devious mind now? 'No, I won't.'

Reaching across, he seized her wrist — the undamaged one — and with no apparent effort jerked her down into the chair. She sat, nursing the new bruises which had not yet had time to appear, and giving him a look of smouldering defiance.

'Now, write.' He flicked a pen towards her.

'What?' she snapped. 'My life-story? Or all the things I hope someone — one dark night — will do to you?'

'Sorrel.' He spoke very softly, but a little drop of ice-water trickled down her spine. 'You have provoked me quite enough. For your own good, do not try my patience any further. You will write.' He picked up the pen and inserted it between her stiff fingers. 'Dear Victoria — '

So he'd found that out. But how stupid — for a man who controlled the financial destiny of an entire nation, discovering the name of her maid would have been child's play.

'Dear Victoria,' he repeated. 'I shall not be returning for several days as I am staying with — what shall we say? — an old friend.' Her lips tightening, she glanced up to meet his sardonic gaze. 'So will you please get together some of my clothes and — '

'Never. I won't write another word of this.' She flung the pen down on the table and folded her arms.

'Very well.' He shrugged. So she'd won — this round, at least. 'If you are perfectly happy to spend your days — and nights — here with me, wearing nothing but that sheet — or less, well . . . '

As he spread his hands Sorrel shot him a look of pure, unadulterated loathing. How could she have been such a fool? Of course she needed clothes. The mere thought of existing wrapped in this horrible sheet, which yet again she could feel slipping down — Furiously she hitched it up, and refastened it so tightly that it cut into her armpits.

And besides, her wrap would have been found by now, abandoned on the beach. That brief verbal message about her staying out to dinner — people might soon begin to wonder if there was something more sinister going on. And she couldn't bear that — Victoria in tears . . . anxious phone calls to London . . . She snatched up the pen.

'Is that it, then?' She scowled up at him.

'Just your signature,' he replied

smoothly, and she scrawled her name across the bottom of the page. 'Ah, beautifully timed,' he added and, from beyond the fringe of bamboos, she caught the sound of a motor.

'Your messenger boy, I suppose,' she said nastily. 'You were very confident he'd have something to deliver, weren't you?'

'Of course.' Sliding the note into an envelope, he said curtly, 'Stay here.' But then, on the top step of the veranda, he turned back. 'On second thoughts, I prefer you where I can see you. Come with me.'

'Are you sure you don't want me to bark as well?' When he looked at her enquiringly, she snarled, ''Stay here' — 'Come with me'. I'm not a poodle, you know.'

'Maybe not, but you will obey me.'

Defiantly she moved an inch further back into the chair, but then paused. At the moment the swine held every card — she was utterly helpless. Well, let him think that she accepted that and then, possibly — though with this man it wasn't wise to assume anything — he just might be lulled into relaxing his guard.

'All right, I'm coming,' she said meekly, and walked past him, but not before she had caught a glimpse of his narrow-eyed scrutiny.

The launch was already gliding alongside the small wooden jetty when they reached the beach. Matt put a hand on her arm and swung her round to face him.

'One more thing. Don't try your wide-eyed act on Carlos. He is very susceptible to the charms of a pretty face.' His eyes swept dispassionately over her features, finally coming to rest on her full mouth, the slightly parted lips. 'And body,' he added, his cool gaze continuing down over her slender frame, its curves enhanced rather than masked by the tightly knotted sheet. 'So don't have any thoughts about him staging a rescue of a — maiden — ' there was an unpleasant inflexion on the word ' — in distress.'

'Oh, you needn't worry,' she snapped. 'I'm sure no errand boy of yours would ever dare risk incurring your displeasure.'

'Perhaps you are right,' he agreed laconically.

'Tell me, do you enjoy terrifying everyone who's unfortunate enough to come into contact with you?'

'Oh, not everyone. Just those whom it gives me a certain amount of pleasure to — terrify.'

'You're a sadist — you know that? A real, twenty-four carat sadist.'

He lifted one careless shoulder. 'If you say so.' He paused. 'Do I terrify you, my sweet?'

He was watching her with clinical detachment, as if she were the latest insect impaled on a pin for his inspection.

'No, you don't,' she retorted. 'Not in the least.'

'How disappointing. I see I shall have to — Ah, Carlos.'

He turned as the young man in white uniform came up to them, his brisk manner not quite veiling his curiosity as he eyed Sorrel's sheet. Matt went to hand him the note, then passed it to her instead.

'You give it to him — it is your letter.'

'That's a nice little sadist's touch,' she said through her teeth, then, conscious of Carlos's speculative glance going from one to the other, flashed him a dazzling smile and held out the envelope.

He took it, looking slightly dazed from the after-shock of that smile, but then met a pair of sardonic green eyes and hastily stuffed it into his jacket pocket. The two men had a rapid conversation — mostly Matt talking, and Carlos listening in acquiescence — then with a brief nod at her Carlos turned away.

He was going off across the beach, to Barbados — to freedom. Suddenly Sorrel was filled with a desperation which was almost frantic to be on that launch, roaring away from this place. Away from Matt.

'Please, Matt.' He was already walking back up the beach but he halted reluctantly, and waited for her to come level with him. 'Please — let me go.' She put a tentative hand on his arm. 'I — I'll make you any promise you like, if you just . . . '

Her voice tailed away to nothing as he looked down at her, his face set in implacable lines.

'You'll promise? Please, don't insult my intelligence.'

'All right, damn you, I won't.' There was no mercy in that hard face. She could grovel on the sand in front of him and he'd just walk on over her. But she wouldn't give him that pleasure.

As he turned away she hitched up the sheet and dropped down on to a driftwood log. The crunching footsteps receded and she stared morosely across the blue-green expanse to where the launch, no more than a white dot now, with a lacy V of foam churning behind it, had almost disappeared over the horizon.

Her left foot was throbbing uncomfortably. She pressed down on the pink sole, peering at a small, uneven tear. It must be where, on her trek round the cay, she'd trodden on that old sea-urchin shell. She'd thought she'd pulled out all of the broken spine, but she must have left a piece.

She was half-heartedly prodding at the cut when, without warning, a pair of tanned legs appeared in her line of vision.

'What is the matter with you?'

'Nothing — absolutely nothing.'

She went to scramble to her feet, then, trying — too late — to smother a yelp of pain, sank down again.

'For God's sake.' Matt's voice crackled with irritability. 'Just tell me what you've done.'

'If you must know, I stepped on a sea-urchin. I think some of it is still in my foot, but I'm fine.' She bent forward again, her long blonde hair swinging round her face. 'So there's absolutely no need for you to worry about me.'

'I'm not,' he said grimly. 'I'm worrying about myself if it becomes infected.'

'You mean, you might have to take me to hospital? Well, thanks.' She gave a shrill laugh. 'Any minute now, you'll be accusing me of stepping on it on purpose, as a way of getting off this loathsome place.'

'The thought had already crossed my mind,' he snapped. 'It's just the kind of devious scheme you would come up with.'

'Oh, you — you — !'

Without warning, the frustration, the anguish, the trauma of the last few hours simmered up and boiled over. She shot to her feet, and, drawing back her hand, she slapped him hard across the face. His hands came up, so that for an instant she thought he was going to hit her back, and terror at what she had done almost made her pass out again on the spot.

She turned to run, but he caught her by the wrist and swung her up into his arms. As he strode off up the beach she lay still, not daring now to protest, her hair brushing against his bare chest, their bodies so close that through the fine cotton sheet she could feel his heart beating, a rapid irregular rhythm as the anger pulsed through him.

She risked a swift glance at his face, lingered just long enough to take in the set expression, the skin flushed with the effort of controlling his temper — except for the pale blotch over one cheekbone which bore the clear imprint of her palm — then her gaze fell.

'Matt,' she said hesitantly.

'What?' A pair of green eyes studied her briefly.

'I'm sorry,' she went on in a small voice. 'I shouldn't have hit you.'

'No, you shouldn't,' he agreed, the velvet tone not at all masking the steel thread of menace. 'But you won't do it again, will you?'

When they reached the veranda he

dumped her unceremoniously into a lounger chair, then, going down on his haunches, lifted her unwilling foot. He ran his fingers over the sole, pausing when her toes flexed involuntarily with pain and a little whimper was torn out from between her clenched teeth, then he set down her foot again.

'I can see some of the spine still in there. I'll have to get it out.'

'Oh, it'll be all right in the morning, I'm sure,' she said hastily.

'Stay there.'

He went off through the green mesh door and came back with a bowl of warm water, a long swirl of antiseptic turning it cloudy white.

'Put your foot in that,' he ordered curtly, then disappeared again, returning with a first-aid box and a towel over his arm.

Going down on his haunches again, in front of her, he briskly dried her foot then took a pair of tweezers and began probing the painful area. Beads of sweat broke out on her forehead but she clenched her whole body so that not a sound should escape her. He must have felt a tremor, though, for he glanced up.

'Am I hurting you?'

'No,' she replied shakily. 'Y-you're very gentle.'

'Not always.' His voice was brusque. 'I can be very — ungentle sometimes.'

As their eyes met she went on quickly, 'You should have been a doctor, not a banker.'

'Actually, I wanted to be one,' he said wryly. 'But that would have taken years of study in the States. So, as my family hadn't a cent, at thirteen I became a messenger boy at the local branch of the Bank of Tierranueva.'

'I see.'

What untold story lay behind his laconic words — of the impoverished thirteen-year-old now head of that same bank? What drive — what ruthless ambition? How many people had he crushed into atoms in that relentless rise to power? A shiver of fear rippled over her skin and he paused again.

'Sorry. There's just one more piece which I'll have to dig for, I'm afraid.'

As she sat back, holding on to the arms of the chair, he shifted slightly to keep his balance. Sorrel looked down at him, her eyes drawn against her will to his shoulders. How smooth they were, like brown silk — smooth and warm to the touch . . . Her gaze shied away in alarm, only to fasten instead on his haunches. The faded denim was stretched as the muscles of his thighs tensed slightly under the effort of staying in that position, and his inner thighs were sprinkled with tiny dark hairs — the same hairs as ran down his belly to disappear under the tight waistband . . .

Her face burning, her heart hammering in her ears, Sorrel's guilty eyes shot upwards — no further, though, than his dark head. Those few grey hairs didn't detract from his looks; in fact, when he went completely grey, then white, he'd be even more devastating, she thought, with a vicious twist of that old pain.

His eyes were lowered, their thick

lashes screening them, and he was frowning slightly in concentration.

'Got it!'

There was a final red-hot needle of pain as he drew out the last remnants of spine, but Sorrel barely felt it. The longing to bend forward and rest her hand on his hair, to caress his face softly, to have him snatch her up in his arms and make passionate love to her was almost overwhelming . . .

Ashen-faced, she went on staring down at him as finally she knew the truth. She'd asked herself often enough in the last five years why she had never been able to make a deep physical commitment to any man. There had been only one man, and he was in her dreams — and, yes, her fantasies. She was always on a sea-shore, the waves pounding inexorably to her very feet, and each time he'd come to her in shadow, dappled in pale silver moonlight, so that she had never once seen his face. A fantasy, but potent enough to imprison her with him forever in that sensual, erotic dream.

How could she not have known, when at times she'd even found herself wishing that on that dreadful night Matt *had* slaked his anger on her, possessing her fully, even violently? What a fool she'd been — a blind fool. Now, though, she'd woken. Her fantasy lover had burst through the dark gauzy web of her dreams into warm, living reality. He was Matt.

4

'More wine?'

Across the table, the silence between them had dragged on for so long that Sorrel gave a start as Matt's clipped voice broke into her thoughts.

'What?' She looked up, and for a moment, as she met his eyes directly for the first time during the meal, the tension inside her fizzed up yet again.

'I said, do you want more wine?' He was holding the bottle of white Chilean Cabernet Sauvignon out to her.

'Oh, no, thank you.'

She watched as he refilled his own glass, the silence weaving itself round them again. There was the quiet hum of the electricity generator at the back of the house, the rustle of dry palm fronds, night insects clicking in the tropical dark beyond the veranda where they sat. Otherwise they might have been the only two people at the furthest edge of the universe, under a sky of scarlet and apricot taffeta.

Leaning back in her chair, she went on watching as his lean fingers closed round the stem of his glass, raising it to his lips, then she saw the muscles move slightly in his strong throat as he drank. Watched — and felt the sharp physical awareness of desire uncoil itself in her, heightening every sense, until she was filled to the brim with him. All she had to do was lean across the narrow table and run her fingers over his bare arm, slip them inside his black open-neck shirt to slide across his chest . . .

'I'll get some coffee.' He half pushed back his chair, snapping the insidious spell.

'Not for me, thanks.' Her voice sounded husky, treacherously warm, and she stood up.

'Where are you going?'

'To unpack my things — and then I'm going to bed. I know it's early, but I'm very tired.' She hesitated, then without looking at him, added, 'Good-night,' and walked stiffly into the house and to her room.

Was it only twenty-four hours ago that, under another tropical sunset, she'd gone for that swim, and for the second time in five years met up with Matt Ramirez and had her life jolted roughly off its smooth tracks? It seemed like a century, she thought as she opened her case again, to take out the rest of her clothes.

When Carlos had delivered it she had brought it through here, laid it on the bed and dragged out the first thing she could find — well, almost the first. She'd rejected the yellow low-cut sundress and instead pulled on this white long-sleeved blouse and rose-patterned cotton skirt. Anything, almost, to be out of that hateful sheet.

A fitted wardrobe took up one wall. She slid open the nearest door and began shaking out her clothes and hanging them, very methodically, so as to fill her mind. But as she smoothed down the turquoise voile skirt which she had brought for evenings, with its matching beaded top, she caught sight of something in the shadows at the back of the wardrobe. Stooping, she pulled it out, and holding it up saw that it was a woman's shirt, in fine black silk.

As Sorrel stared at it, unpleasant sensations churning in her stomach, she caught a faint scent which lingered around the collar. She sniffed it. Sakkara, wasn't it? The kind of perfume that only a very poised, intensely sensual woman would choose. And surely, beneath it, very faintly — she pressed the folds to her nose — she could smell the elusive aroma of spice and warm maleness that was Matt . . .

Her hands closed over the shirt and, screwing it into a ball, she hurled it back into its corner.

'You have enough room, I hope.' Sorrel spun round to see Matt lounging in the doorway, a sardonic glint in his pale eyes. 'I can always move some of my things out of your way temporarily.'

'*Your* things? But I thought — '

Breaking off abruptly, she pushed back the far wardrobe door, her eyes widening as she took in the row of hanging T-shirts, jeans, a couple of light linen suits — all unmistakably masculine. Her gaze slid across to the bed, a small double.

'Yes, that's right,' he said easily. 'This is my bedroom.'

But she had slept last night in that bed — his bed.

'I'm sorry.' Sorrel, her cheeks flaring, snatched an armful of clothes out of the wardrobe and flung them back into the case.

'Please, feel free to use it.' Matt held up his hands. 'This is the only wardrobe.'

'Oh.' She hesitated. 'Thanks, but I'll still take them through to the other bedroom.'

'But, you see, there is no other bedroom.'

She gaped at him. 'There's that other door in the lounge.'

'Yes, but that leads to my office. I occasionally have to work, even in my bolt-hole.'

'I see,' she said slowly.

'There are — oh, five or six suites in my villa back on Barbados — I do much of my entertaining there — but when I come here I come alone. At least, most of the time.'

As their eyes met a reminiscent little smile tugged at those thin lips and Sorrel, remembering that black silk shirt, felt another little eddy of pain ripple through her.

'Do use the bathroom first,' he went on casually. 'After all, I am the mere host, you are the guest here.'

'Guest!' The pain found its outlet in bitterness. 'Is that what you call it?'

'But of course,' he replied urbanely. 'How would you describe yourself?'

'Prisoner, of course. Guests are free to come and go as they choose.'

'And, if you could choose, you would walk out of here without a backward glance?'

'Too right, I would,' she retorted.

'Are you quite sure of that, Sorrel?' His voice was wrapped in silk.

'Of course I'm sure.'

All at once, though, he looked so tall, so intimidating in those dark trousers which embraced his long legs and lean, hard thighs, and the black shirt, whose buttons he was beginning to undo . . .

'Wh-what are you doing?' Her voice rose sharply.

'Oh, I think I'll have an early night too.'

'But — ' she ran the tip of her tongue round her lips ' — where are you sleeping?'

'Here, of course. Where else would I sleep?' His eyes were very green tonight — like a cat's, a watchful cat's.

'But I thought — '

'I gave up my bed to you last night, but I really prefer it to the sofa so I have no intention of doing so again. I'm sorry.' He wasn't, though, not in the least. 'You're very welcome to join me, of course. I've always been told I'm the perfect bedfellow.'

'No, I won't, damn you.'

He spread his hands wide in infinite regret. 'In that case, I hope you have a better night than I did — on the sofa.'

She gave him a look of smouldering hatred. 'If you were halfway a gentleman — '

'Ah, but I'm not, am I? We both know that.' And he undid another of his shirt buttons . . .

When she emerged from the bathroom, tightly belted into her white broderie anglaise housecoat over a matching nightie, he had slung a couple of folded sheets on to the sofa together with a brightly coloured Indian rug. Tight-lipped, she shook them out to make herself a rough bed then, after switching off the lights, slipped out of her housecoat and slid between the sheets.

She lay rigid as Matt's shadowy form, apparently enclosed in very little, went through to the bathroom. The water began cascading in the tiny shower, and suddenly she was fighting ineffectually to blot out from her mind the image of that body, the droplets gleaming on the skin, catching in the tiny black hairs on his chest and trickling down his belly and thighs.

As she swallowed hard the door opened and Matt reappeared, a small towel slung low on his hips. Silhouetted against the light, he seemed even more menacing, and she shrank slightly into the sofa, her fingers clutching on the sheet.

He crossed the room and stood looking down at her, his face a dark mask in the half-light. Sorrel felt the tension coiling even tighter in her until finally, just as the scream of near-hysteria was erupting to the surface, he said, 'Goodnight. Oh — and sleep well.'

'Don't worry, I will,' she snarled, and the bedroom door closed on a soft laugh . . .

★ ★ ★

Two hours later, for the hundredth time, she flung herself despairingly on to her other side. She might just as well have downed a gallon of black coffee, for she was going to lie here, wide awake, until morning. It was all the fault of this horrible sofa — and of that swine, dead to the world, no doubt, in his luxurious bed.

He'd be sprawled there, his dark head on the pillow, naked — for Matt surely wouldn't tolerate the restriction of pyjamas — that lithe, beautiful body covered only by a sheet. Or maybe the sheet had slid off when she'd heard him turn over half an hour ago, disturbed by that shutter which had rattled in a sudden gust of wind . . .

Oh, Lord. Sorrel writhed, trying desperately to blot out those images which flickered like a silent movie behind her eyelids. No. She couldn't blame this sofa. What was keeping her awake was the blinding revelation which had put a face to her fantasy, and the knowledge that the sexual attraction — on her side at least — was as strong now as it had been at their very first

110

meeting five years ago.

She buried her hot face in the cushion with a groan. How was she going to survive whole days — and nights — alone with him? But she had to — had to fight her feelings, her longings, for there was no future for her with Matt. 'I thought I was in love with you,' he'd said once, but he'd cut through the fragile bonds with no remorse, no regret.

Her lids began to droop, opened wide, then fell again . . .

Once more she was on a beach, but this time it was the beach on the cay and she was pushing her way through the overgrown bamboo, its dry leaves scratching at her skin like fingernails. Under the pale tropical moonlight the sand was a strange, unearthly silver, and it was soft under her bare feet. The sea was rough — she could hear its dull booming and see, far out, the wall of breakers crawling endlessly towards her.

She walked down to that dark line where the sea met the land. As she knelt the water foamed over her nakedness, patterning her flesh like white lace, and gradually she sank down in it. Beyond the reef the waves were still thundering, and a line of white sea-horses were moving to the shore. They seemed to rear themselves up over her, the opaque gleam on the underwave glinting like metal as the moon's rays caught it.

Then, as she watched, spellbound, he came — as he always did. The water parted and one of those sea-horses came plunging through, straight as an arrow towards her. There was no time for fear; the horse was almost on her before she saw, low on its back, fingers twined in its flying mane, the dark rider.

The horse reared, then halted almost at her feet and stood, tossing its head and snorting as the spray broke round it. The rider sat, looking silently down at her where she lay at his feet, then dismounted, tossing the reins over the stallion's back. He stood over her, his body gleaming silver, his face — as always — hidden by his mount's arching back.

The blood was roaring in her ears, drowning the crash of breakers, as she held out her arms to him. Then, as he came down to her, his face moved from shadow into moonlight — and it was Matt.

His eyes were very pale, like green ice, and a small, cruel smile played round his thin lips.

'Hello, Sorrel.' It was his voice — velvety, husky. 'Women like you need to be taught a lesson . . . taught a lesson . . . taught a lesson . . . '

'No.' He was coming down on her and, stumbling upright, she tried to run. But her feet sank in the damp sand and his hands were reaching out to take her. 'No! No!'

'What the hell — ?'

A wall-light flicked on, blotting out the silvery moonlight and those frozen figures, and as her dazed eyes jerked open they took in Matt, standing in the doorway, dragging a black towelling robe over his naked body. As he swiftly crossed the room towards her he came between her and the light, so that his face was in shadow, and in that split-second dream and reality fused and became one.

'No — no!' Sorrel, her hands shaking, tried to ward him off. 'Don't touch me.'

'For God's sake — are you ill?'

He moved to take hold of her, but, almost out of her mind with terror, she sprang up from the sofa and wriggled free of his outstretched arms. But when she reached the door a shriek was torn from her as a pair of strong hands seized her, swinging her round.

'Let me go!' She fought like a crazy thing, throwing punches in all directions. 'Leave me alone.'

One flailing fist caught the side of his jaw, and, muttering some obscenity, he dragged her into his arms. Before she could protest or scream his lips came down on hers, silencing her, smothering all sound except their laboured breathing. His fingers were tangling roughly in her hair and tears of pain blurred her eyes as he held her face to his.

She swayed on her feet and he drew her closer into him — so close, their bodies separated only by the flimsy nightie and his robe, that she felt the scorching heat from every line of him, felt his body quicken with sudden sexual hunger while his greedy mouth ravished hers. Stiff-tongued, he thrust into her mouth until she was forced to yield to him, giving up her sweetness as he plundered her mercilessly. Her head was whirling, brilliant colours flashing in her brain, as sensations crushed for so long leapt into brilliant life.

This was her dream, that fantasy which had fed her for five famished years — Matt, become reality — and she was holding him in her arms, so warm and vibrant and overpowering that she ached to surrender herself to him.

But no! Reality was a man who despised her, who called her 'tramp' and 'whore'.

Wrenching her mouth free, so violently that fine strands of her hair were caught in his fingers, she gasped, 'Leave me alone, I tell you.'

His grip tightened even more for a moment, so that terror surged through her again, but then it slackened and he looked down at her, at first as though he hardly saw her as she stood, her breast heaving, gulping air into her parched lungs.

But then he gave her an odd, crooked smile. 'Well, well, my sweet.' His voice was almost — not wholly — under control. 'It seems I am not quite so immune to your charms as I thought. I can hardly deny what my body so clearly tells you, can I?'

'Don't be so crude,' she said coldly, but he raised one dark brow.

'Is it crude to say that I physically desire a beautiful woman? Surely not — and especially not when that woman is you.'

He raised one hand to caress her flushed cheek, but she jerked her head back again.

116

'There's no physical desire on my part, I assure you,' she retorted fiercely. 'Especially when the man in question is you. I loved you once, Matt. Yes.' His thin lips had curled cynically. 'And you turned that love to hate. But I'm over that now — all I feel for you is utter indifference.'

'Hmm. I wonder.'

He was studying her with blatant insolence, his eyes raking over her body, its slender curves barely concealed beneath the cotton. To her horror, she felt her breasts stir, as though under a slow, erotic caress, and, glancing down, saw her nipples thrusting against the light fabric. As she looked up, her eyes wide and helpless, she saw that Matt too had seen, and that his sensual mouth was curving into a feral smile.

'Surely, my dear Sorrel, we can come to some — arrangement while we remain here. Profitable to you, of course — I would not expect it to be otherwise.'

She bit on her inner mouth until she

tasted salty blood. How could he be so cruel, so vindictive?

'I'm sorry — ' she raised her head proudly ' — but there's nothing you could offer me that would persuade me to sleep with you.'

'You think not?' His voice dropped to a low purr, and she was powerless to move as, lifting one hand, he caught a strand of pale silky hair between his fingers. 'You know, there would have been a certain piquancy in lovemaking with a nineteen-year-old — at least — ' his lips twisted ' — while I thought I was the first to have that privilege.' As she tried to look down his fingers tightened, forcing her head up until her eyes met his. 'Now, though, you are five years older, and no doubt five years more accomplished in the arts of pleasing a lover.'

'You really are a swine.' Her voice shook. 'You never go for anything less than the jugular, do you?'

'Of course not,' he agreed smoothly. 'What else is there to go for?'

'But let me tell you something. There's no way I would ever — ever — make love with you.' She drew an angry, shuddering breath. 'You humiliated me once. But then, humiliation is the name of the game for you, isn't it, Matt?'

As his brows snapped down she went on defiantly, 'You talk about five years ago. Well, five years is a long time — long enough for me not to be the same Sorrel Elliot.'

'But suppose I am the same Matt Ramirez?'

She gave a bitter laugh. 'Oh, you are, believe me.'

'And that magnetism between our two bodies, pulling us together, is still the same. It was there from the first day we met, and it is here now, so that all I have to do is wait.'

'Wait?' Her voice was brittle. 'Since when were you ever prepared to wait for anything?'

'How well you know me, Sorrel,' he agreed urbanely. 'And it is, sadly, only a matter of days before our — island idyll comes to an end. So you are quite right. Why should we wait?'

As he moved to take her in his arms again the V of his robe fell apart, revealing even more of that strong chest, with the whorls of black hair against the satin skin. The robe was tightly belted but this only heightened the long line of his narrow flanks and legs, bare to the thigh.

There was a tightness in her throat and the blood hummed in her ears, but, her fingers clenching rigidly with the effort to subdue the treacherous surge of emotion, she jerked away from him.

'You still think I'm a little whore.' The monosyllable seared her mouth like acid. 'You're so wrong about that — not that I expect you to believe it, of course.'

'I'm so glad,' he sneered.

Useless. It was quite useless trying to convince him. He was remorseless in his view of her — remorseless and unforgiving. So she would have to fight him on his own terms — the only terms he understood.

'And one way you're wrong is in that these days I'm choosy who I go to bed with.' The distasteful words almost choked in her throat, but somehow she met his sardonic gaze head-on. 'You said I was prepared to use my body for what I could get out of you. Well, now you've found me out there's nothing in it for me from sleeping with you. So — sorry, Matt.' With a last supreme effort she made her voice as careless and unfeeling as his own. 'Nothing doing.'

He stood there for a long moment, regarding her, his green eyes narrowed.

'A pretty speech, my love — and almost convincing. Not quite, though.'

Before she could move, he raised a lazy hand and brushed it just once around her lips. Their skin barely touched, and yet she felt the shiver of excitement run through her whole body in answer to that instantaneous physical tug between them.

'You see?' Derision glinted in his pale eyes. 'All I have to do is wait — but not for very long, I'm sure.'

With a last mocking little smile, he thrust his hands into his pockets and sauntered back to his room. In the doorway, he paused.

'By the way, what was all that yelling about? Were you having a dream or something?'

'More of a nightmare, actually,' she replied tightly. 'But don't worry, Matt. I'm quite sure I shan't be having it again.'

5

Her pink bikini was the first thing Sorrel saw when she opened her eyes. It was draped just at eye-level across a chair which had been placed beside the sofa. Very amusing. She regarded it sourly, then, hearing footsteps outside on the veranda, went tense in every limb, staring at the door.

But the steps faded, and when, very cautiously, she eased herself off the sofa and went across to the window, she saw Matt heading for the beach. He had a towel round his neck and was wearing black swimming briefs which, slung low on his hips, moulded themselves to his body. Unconscious of her eyes on him, he walked with that easy, lithe grace, natural arrogance in every line of the way he held himself.

Plunging into the screen of bamboo, he disappeared, and Sorrel, realising that she had been greedily devouring that superb body with her eyes, angrily caught herself up and went off to the bathroom.

She deliberately took a very long time over her shower, and when she came out on to the veranda, wearing a crisp white sleeveless blouse and peach-coloured linen shorts, he was seated at the old pine table where they had eaten dinner. There was a dark blue enamel coffee-pot at his elbow, a wicker basket of luscious-looking fruit and some rolls — removed earlier from the big chest freezer in the kitchen, presumably.

He was sitting with his back to her, studying an open file and tapping a pen against it in concentration. His hair was still damp, and above the light blue T-shirt he had put on it curled into his nape. Rather endearing, Sorrel thought — until, that was, you reminded yourself who that nape and softly curling hair belonged to.

The veranda was shaded by the pale coralita vine and morning glory, which sprawled all over it and hung its sky-blue flower-heads down through the wooden slats. A couple of iridescent humming-birds were skimming to and fro, plunging their beaks in ecstasy among the scarlet petals of a hibiscus bush. On the top step an emerald gecko lizard was basking, lifting its orange throat to the sun, and through the clumps of oleander and bamboo she glimpsed the Caribbean, its turquoise surface unruffled in the still morning air.

The perfect setting for — what had Matt so caustically termed it? — an island idyll. Perfect, too, for a lovers' hideaway. All at once, the scene before her blurred and shimmered. If, on that dreadful night five years ago, Matt had asked her to marry him, maybe they would have come here, just the two of them, lost in the joy of discovering one another. They'd have walked hand in hand, swum together, laughed together, and each night lain in each other's arms in his bedroom, with just the sound of the sea shushing softly on to that heart-achingly lovely beach . . .

He glanced briefly over his shoulder. 'Good morning. Sleep well?'

'Morning.' She blinked away the moistness in her eyes. 'Yes, thank you.' Though in reality she had been still awake when the first streaks of dawn had showed through the wooden shutters.

'That's good.'

He kicked back the chair opposite him and she slid into it. He was wearing dark glasses, and the fact that he was coolly surveying her while his own expression remained invisible increased her uneasiness — putting her at the disadvantage it was no doubt meant to, she thought resentfully. He poured a cup of coffee and pushed it across to her.

'Thank you,' she said coolly. 'I trust you enjoyed your swim.'

'Very much.'

'No sharks?' she enquired sweetly. Apart from one, of course — but she kept that thought to herself.

'None that I noticed,' he replied evenly. 'I always have a jog — and a swim too, if I can. It's a great way to start the day.'

'And then you go out and eat people.'

She gave him a spiked smile and, taking a roll, spread it with butter and some of the pale amber-coloured guava jelly.

'If I'm hungry enough, yes.'

His tone was still perfectly level, but as she took a sip of coffee she felt the tension spiral in her. It really wasn't very clever to be baiting Matt, but it seemed the only possible safety valve for her inner turmoil. It was no help, of course, that he was perfectly relaxed this morning, as if that fraught scene a few hours earlier had never happened. He was so damned sure of himself — so sure that she would fall into his hands as easily as one of those ripe papaws in the basket beside him.

'You must join me tomorrow morning.' His tone was bland. 'Now that that elegant little bikini of yours has miraculously reappeared.'

'I had noticed,' she replied woodenly, giving all her attention to slicing through a papaw then carefully scraping every one of the jet-black seeds from its pinky-gold centre.

Draining his coffee, he closed the heavy file with a snap and got to his feet. He stood looking down at her, but, suddenly aware of that muscular body, his tanned thighs visible now beneath his white shorts, she kept her eyes fixed on her plate. One seed, two seeds, three seeds —

'I shall be busy all day. I have a lot of work to do.'

'Oh?' Neatly she cut a slice of papaw, the drops of golden nectar spurting out. 'I thought this was your bolt-hole.'

'So it is, but I wasn't planning on using it just now,' he added grimly.

'And what am I supposed to do?'

Out of the corner of her eye she saw him lift one shoulder — a careless shrug which set her teeth on edge.

'Continue your convalescence. Swim, sunbathe — whatever you wish.'

'Not *quite* everything, surely?' she snapped. 'I can't sell that world scoop story to the highest bidder, can I?'

'No.' His voice crispened a fraction. 'You cannot do that, my sweet. But otherwise you have the freedom of the island.'

'Freedom?' She stabbed viciously at the papaw. 'Thanks very much.'

He picked up the file and tucked it under his arm. 'Help yourself to anything you fancy for lunch. I shan't bother till tonight.'

★   ★   ★

At noon, when Sorrel reluctantly went back to the white-board beach-house after a morning of solitary swimming and sunbathing, there was no sign of Matt. In the kitchen, she opened the freezer but found herself faced with a bewildering array of exotic pre-cooked dishes. Bolt-hole maybe, but he certainly didn't believe in the simple life as far as food was concerned, she thought ironically as she homed in instead on the stack of tins in one of the bleached wood wall-cupboards.

Even these, though, seemed to consist mainly of foie gras, truffled chicken and peaches in white wine — a long way from the baked beans and pilchards which filled her store cupboard, at least when times were hard. Finally she chose a tin of tongue, made a pile of sandwiches and a salad, then loaded up a tray, complete with a glass of milk and a couple of rosy nectarines.

When she opened the door of Matt's office half a hair's-breadth, he was seated at a desk, scowling morosely across a sea of papers at the opposite wall. His thick hair was standing on end where he'd obviously been running his fingers through it over and over.

Quietly she set down the tray, but he ignored it and her, and she had reached the door when his caustic voice halted her.

'I thought I said I wasn't eating till tonight.'

'I know you did,' she said tightly. 'But I was getting lunch for myself and thought you might like some. Don't worry, though — I'll take it away again.'

But as she reached for the tray a hand slapped down on it.

'You may as well leave it, now it's here,' he muttered ungraciously.

Sorrel hesitated, fighting down the urge to snatch the tray and up-end it all over him, but then, as she was turning away, her eye fell on a loose sheet of paper at his elbow, covered in elaborate doodles. The mega-powered international banker, a secret doodler . . . She smiled to herself at this sign of ordinary human weakness in a man who seemed no more than a ruthless machine, then, on a sudden overwhelming impulse, she slid out her hand to capture the paper for herself.

'What the hell are you doing with that?'

Matt's eyes, all at once ice-sharp,

were trained on her, cold accusation in them.

'S-sorry.' Two bright spots of colour stung her cheeks. 'I didn't realise doodles were top secret, as well as everything else on this loathsome island.' And, swinging on her heel, she stalked out, slamming the door so that every wooden shutter rattled.

As angry, hurt tears scalded her eyes she grabbed her own tray and took it out on to the veranda. But the food remained untasted for long minutes as she sat, willing the flock of tiny red butterflies fluttering among the morning glory flowers overhead to soothe away the pain . . .

*　*　*

Something fell softly on to her stomach. Lifting her head, she saw that it was a mauve flower-head from the oleander bush which was shading her from the mid-afternoon sun. She sat up, twirling it round between her fingers and gazing abstractedly across the creamy sand to the sea, a dazzle of aquamarine.

What was she going to do? A simple page of Matt's scribbles could twist her heartstrings into knots, his eyes, filled with ice-cold suspicion, could make that same heart ache like a bruise, and his fingers, brushing softly across her lips, could set up sensations within her that surely she could not deny for much longer . . .

Far out at sea, a small white-sailed yacht was tacking to and fro in the gentle afternoon breeze, and she watched it listlessly. Where was it going? The Careenage, that bustling marina she'd wandered around in downtown Bridgetown, perhaps?

Sorrel's dark blue eyes, which had been vague and unfocused, widened suddenly. What on earth was she thinking of? Leaping to her feet, she ran to the water's edge and, after one swift glance over her shoulder, began waving both arms frantically. But the little boat serenely kept to its course.

133

Almost beside herself now, she raced back up the sand, snatched up her oversize white voile shirt and hurtled up on to the low headland at the far end of the beach. Sobbing for breath, she stood waving the shirt with one hand and beckoning frenziedly with the other.

Oh, please — *please* come. In silent desperation — she dared not call out for fear of Matt hearing her — she willed the yacht to her. It had almost sailed out of sight when, nearly weeping with frustration, she saw a tiny hand wave, and then the boat veered round and began making for the shore.

Back on the beach, Sorrel scrambled everything into her straw bag, and by the time the yacht was into the shallows she was already wading out to it. She looked up, to see three young men in baseball caps and sawn-off denims regarding her.

'Hi!' one called.

'Er — hi.'

Confronted with their unashamedly

appreciative gazes, taking in every centimetre of her, she faltered, wishing that she'd taken another few seconds to put on her shirt over her bikini. But any qualms were overwhelmed by the desperate need to be away from Matt.

'Are you — ?' Her voice was tight with tension. She cleared her throat and began again. 'Are you going to Bridgetown?'

'Sure.' Three pairs of openly curious eyes were fixed on her as she stood, the water swirling round her knees.

'Well, could you give me a lift? I — I need to get back. I'll — '

'This island is private property.'

At the clipped words every head swung round, and Sorrel gave a gasp of sheer terror at the sight of Matt striding down the beach towards them. She stared, frozen.

'*Please.*'

But even as she turned imploringly to the men Matt's arm snaked round her waist, pulling her to him. She tried to jerk away, but his grip tightened in silent warning.

'So I'd be grateful if you'd move on,' he continued smoothly.

'You would, would you?' A well-built youth with flaming red hair retorted. 'And who says this place is private?'

'I do.' Two words, but they were enough. The three men eyed Matt for a moment longer, clearly taking his measure, then the red-haired one shrugged.

'OK, OK — we're going. But the young lady here — ' he favoured Sorrel with a hostile glance ' — she seemed pretty keen for us to come in.'

'Oh, darling.' For the first time Matt looked directly at her. The tender, protective little smile was for the benefit of their audience; his eyes were about as warm as a glacier in mid-winter. 'I really thought you were getting over it.'

'What do you mean — getting over it?' She looked at him in bewilderment.

'The first unsuspecting young men who come within reach. Oh, dear.' He shook his head sadly.

'Now, look here.' Sorrel's face flamed

with temper. 'You just — '

'It's so unfortunate.' He addressed the yachtsmen, who were now, she realised with baffled rage, almost literally backing away from her. 'She really cannot help herself, I'm afraid.'

Tenderly he brushed aside a lock of blonde hair which had fallen across her hot forehead, and she had to fight against the impulse to bite his hand.

'It's her hormones,' he went on urbanely. 'We — '

'Oh, for — ' Crimson with embarrassment now, she tried to interrupt but he overrode her.

'We — her doctors and I — thought she was responding so well to the treatment.'

'Don't believe him!' All too well aware that the moment the yacht had gone the smooth façade of loving concern would crack wide open to reveal the incandescent fury which was already searing the bare flesh where his hand gripped her, Sorrel threw discretion to the winds. 'He's keeping me here because . . . '

But as Matt's grasp tightened even more, his fingers biting into her skin, her voice tailed limply away. The feeling of utter powerlessness which so often took control of her when he was around washed over her now. He intended her to stay on this island, so there was no power on earth that would get her off it.

And in any case, his suave international-man-of-the-world act was having far more of an effect on the men than ever she, a mere hysterical woman — and a rabid man-eater at that — could hope to achieve. Under the force of his personality, their belligerence had faded entirely, so that she even thought she glimpsed a complicit male glance pass between them over her head.

'Well, enjoy your sail,' Matt concluded with a warm smile.

'Thanks. Cheers.'

Sorrel stood motionless, still bound by that arm clamped round her, and watched as they turned into the wind. The sail flapped, then as the breeze caught it the yacht skimmed away.

When at last she risked a glance at Matt from under her lashes his face was very pale, except for two lines of dark colour on his sharp-edged cheekbones. She made a convulsive movement to break free, but he caught her by the wrist and dragged her out of the water, hard up against him.

'What the hell do you think you were playing at?' he snarled into her face.

'What did it look like?' She tossed back her hair defiantly. 'And what do you think — ?'

'You'll do anything to get that world scoop, won't you?'

'World scoop?' In her frantic urgency to get away, that had been completely wiped from her mind. 'No, of course — '

Oh, what was the use? What was ever the use with this man? She gave a careless shrug. 'Of course I would. Well, Matt, put yourself in my place.'

He expelled a furious breath, then said with barely controlled savagery, 'So you'd risk getting into a boat with three unknown men — '

'They were perfectly harmless — unlike some I could mention.'

'Really? When I came on the scene they were looking at you as if you were their next meal, honey.'

'They were not,' she burst out heatedly.

'It's lucky for you that I decided you'd been left to your own devices for long enough. You should be grateful I stepped in.'

'Grateful!'

'To save you from yourself.'

'Not every man is like you, you know.' Her eyes spat blue fire. 'Some are decent, honourable — '

'Gentlemen, you mean?' His lip curled.

'Exactly. You may not believe it, but there actually are some men around who don't regard every woman as their lawful prey.'

'You amaze me,' he jeered. 'And just how were you planning to repay those *gentlemen* for their trouble? With your usual currency, I presume — a taste of that delectable body.'

'Oh!' All the air was knocked out of her, as though he had punched her in the solar plexus. 'How dare you?'

'Oh, I dare, my sweet. I dare.'

'You — you really enjoyed that little scene, didn't you?'

'Did I?'

'All you had to do was say, 'Sorry, there's been a misunderstanding', and they'd have gone, with their tails between their legs. You have that effect on people, you see — you scare them half to death.'

'I'm so glad to hear that.'

'In fact, they *were* going — but you couldn't leave it at that, could you? You had to make them think that I'm some kind of raging nymphomaniac.'

'They didn't seem to need much persuading.' And at the studied insolence in his voice she had to clench her nails into her palms to quell the desire to spring at him and claw away that derisive sneer.

'Y-you humiliated me yet again.'

'You have only yourself to blame,' he replied coldly. 'I made it perfectly clear that I intend you to stay here, and I do not allow my intentions to be thwarted.'

'All right, all right,' she snapped. 'Message received.'

Taking a tight hold of her beach-bag, she turned away, but he gave her other wrist a jerk which brought her back to face him.

'Where do you think you're going now?'

'To swim. Any objections?'

'Plenty. You're staying where I can see you from now on — which means at the house.'

'No, I'm not.' She tossed her bag down. 'I'll have my swim, and then I'll come back to the house.' And to make her point she dropped on to the sand beside her bag.

'You little — ' His features tight with anger, he bit off the word, but Sorrel's stomach had time for just one quick, terrified lurch as he made a grab at her.

She tried to roll away, but he pounced on her.

'Come here, you!'

Snatching her up, he half dragged, half carried her across the beach, struggling and kicking all the way, and finally dumped her — hard — in a bamboo chair on the veranda. He wiped the back of his arm across his brow, where the exertion had brought out beads of sweat, then stood over her, hands on hips, breathing deeply.

'If you know what's good for you, stay put.'

'No, I won't.'

She glowered up at him, then, to underline her defiance, gripped the arms of the chair to lever herself upright. He pushed her back down and held her pinned by the shoulders, his furious green eyes very close to hers.

'If you try to get out of that chair again, so help me, I'll tie you into it for the rest of the day.' He paused, then, obviously struggling to gain control of his temper, added a fraction more calmly, 'Do you hear me?'

'Yes, yes, yes!' she yelled in his face. 'I hear you, you swine.'

'Good.'

Straightening up, he went off through the green mesh door then came back with a pile of books. Hooking across a small table with his foot, he set them down beside her.

'Something for you to read.'

'Oh, yes? *Economics for Beginners*, I suppose.'

'Actually, I don't keep financial books out here,' he replied evenly. 'They're thrillers.' He dropped *The Day of the Jackal* into her lap.

'Sorry, I don't like thrillers.' Sorrel folded her arms and stared stubbornly out to sea.

'In that case, can you play patience?'

'Might do,' she muttered.

'Well — ' he slapped a brand new deck of cards on top of the books ' — play it, then.'

Going across to the pine table where his papers were spread, weighed down by a beautiful pink conch shell and a lump of creamy-white coral, he sat down, his back to her, and immersed himself immediately in his work.

Sorrel, her mouth compressed, stared at that back for several minutes, then, dragging across the small metal table, she pushed aside the pile of paperbacks and opened up the cards, setting them out for patience . . .

★　★　★

Yet another game that wasn't going to come out. She scowled down at the rows of brightly coloured cards in front of her, then morosely flung down the three of hearts again, scooped the whole pack together and got to her feet.

'What do you think you're doing?'

She could have sworn that she hadn't made a sound, but Matt's abrasive voice halted her in her tracks.

'Don't worry,' she snapped as his head turned. 'I'm only going to get a cold drink. Any objections?'

'Get me one as well.'

'Lime juice on crushed ice, twist of orange, I presume?'

He nodded approvingly. 'That's it. I like my women to know my tastes.'

'I am *not* your — ' But he had already turned back to his work.

In the kitchen she flicked on the juicer, then stood glaring down at it, wishing that it was someone's saturnine face that she was pulping to extinction.

As she set his glass down beside him he stretched with a grimace and flexed his shoulder muscles, stiff after more than two hours of concentrated work. She gazed spellbound at those muscles, rippling beneath the brown satin skin, but when he grunted a 'Thanks', and glanced up at her, she hastily fixed a sweetly saccharine smile in place.

'I trust it's to your satisfaction, sir.'

The smile vanished instantly, though, as she saw that all his papers had been turned over so that only their plain backs were visible.

'I'm amazed you trust me even to get

you a drink,' she said bitterly. 'Aren't you terrified that I might slip something in it?'

'Terrified?' A pair of cool green eyes surveyed her. 'Oh, no, Sorrel, you don't terrify me.'

'What a pity.' Feeble, but all she could manage.

'Yes, it is, isn't it?' he agreed evenly, then, after taking a long gulp of lime juice, glanced meaningfully across at her table. 'Well, back to your game, then.'

'I'm tired of patience.' She aimed a vicious kick at a pretty yellow shell lying innocuously on the polished veranda boarding.

'Play something else, then.'

'I don't know any more card-games for one,' she replied sullenly.

'Yes, well, games for two are always more — entertaining, aren't they?'

'It depends on your opponent,' she muttered, refusing to meet the ironic challenge in his gaze. 'Do you know any card-games?'

He pulled a face. 'They bore me.'

Yes, they would, wouldn't they? she thought. A man as dynamic, as vibrantly physical as Matt would chafe at being confined for long at a card-table.

'Oh, well — ' she gave a resigned little shrug ' — patience it is, then.'

But as she was turning away he pushed his papers aside with an irritable gesture. 'OK, what do you want to play?'

'Oh.' She swung back, only just managing to hide the ridiculous little spurt of joy. Those grudging words were the first sign of anything other than anger or chill contempt that he had shown her since their confrontation on the beach. 'Well, have you got another pack of cards?'

'No.'

'We can't play bezique, then. Hmm.' She wrinkled her brow. 'How about German whist? Two can play that.'

'Whist? No, thanks,' he replied firmly. 'What's that game Paul Newman plays in *The Sting*?'

She stared at him. 'On the train, you mean?' And, when he nodded, she said doubtfully, 'Well, poker.'

'All right, let's play that.'

'But it's not really a game for two.'

'Oh, I'm sure that with your fertile brain we'll manage somehow. Fetch the cards.' As she did so he gathered up his papers and set them on the floor at his feet. 'Right, sit down.'

He gestured peremptorily to the chair facing him, but she hung back. 'Poker's a gambling game.'

'So?'

'I haven't any money with me — thanks to you,' she added pointedly.

'Let's play for IOUs, then. You can make good your losses later.'

Her losses? If he really was such a complete novice at cards she'd be the one to be collecting the winnings. But, no — she dared not take the risk. Anything he lost would be a flea-bite to someone as wealthy as Matt, whereas for her . . .

She looked up, to see his sardonic

gaze on her, but she shook her head firmly.

'No, I'm sorry — I don't play for money.'

'Oh, well, if you're chicken — ' he gave her a sidelong glance ' — back to your patience, then.'

But her eyes fell on the box of matches, still on the table from when Matt had lit the candles at dinner the previous evening.

'When I was at Guide Camp we used to play for matchsticks.'

He raised a black brow. 'Poker? At Guide Camp? What a misspent youth you had, Ms Elliot.'

'But I've more than made up for it since, haven't I?' she retorted, stung by his blatant sarcasm.

'Oh, yes, you have,' he said softly. 'Still — if you insist.' Opening the box, he carefully divided the contents into two equal piles and pushed one across to her. 'Now, how do we start?'

'I'll deal.' Snatching up the cards, she shuffled them with brisk efficiency. 'We

have five cards each, and then you have
to try and . . . '

★   ★   ★

'Is that it, then?'

'Afraid so.' Sorrel gave him a slightly
shame-faced smile. 'It's my game
again.'

With a rueful grimace, he passed
across to her the last of his pathetically
small heap of matches. A pity she
hadn't had the courage to take him up
on that IOU offer. Just think, if each of
those matchsticks had been worth, say,
a thousand dollars . . . Yes, it would
have been deeply satisfying to let him
think she was taking him to the
cleaners. And then, of course —
because she would never touch a cent
of Matt Ramirez's money — she'd have
contemptuously ripped every IOU in
half and tossed them back in his face
. . . Extremely satisfying — but it was
too late now.

'So the game's over?'

151

Sorrel hastily wiped the secret little smile off her lips. 'That's right.' She began scooping her winnings into a tidy pile.

'Unless, of course, you want to raise the stakes.'

She looked across at him, instantly wary. 'How do you mean?'

'Play for something more — exciting. In fact, I reckon that was my problem,' he went on earnestly. 'Somehow matchsticks never have got my adrenalin flowing.'

'What do you suggest?' She eyed him suspiciously. In spite of his bland tone, warning bells were still ringing in her brain.

He shrugged. 'You're the expert. Any ideas?'

She sat back, chewing her lower lip. He wouldn't give her a second chance to play for money, so . . .

'All right,' she said abruptly, 'if you really want to raise the stakes, we'll play one more game. If you win, I promise not to make any more attempts to get away from here.'

'And if I lose?'

'You take me back to Barbados as soon as possible and set me free. What do you say?'

She gazed at him, willing him to give her this chance to be free of him, but he shook his head. 'A clever ploy, my sweet, but no. I hate to turn down a challenge, especially from you, but I am not prepared to risk my country's future on a hand of cards.'

She winced inwardly, and her heart, which had been fluttering with a wild hope, fell back to the pit of her stomach.

'Those secret talks, I suppose you mean? But they're not at risk.' She looked across at him imploringly, her hands twisting together on the table. 'You must believe me, Matt. I give you my word that I shan't tell a living soul about them.'

'Your word? But we both know how much reliance can be placed on that, don't we?'

The clipped words fell from his tongue, forming a dagger of ice which pierced her to her vitals.

'Yes, we do.' To hide the pain that must be showing in her eyes she bent over the table, gathering up the cards, then added stiffly, 'Thank you for the game. And don't worry, I shan't inflict it on you any longer.'

'There is, of course, one other way of raising the stakes.'

At his silky tone her gaze rose involuntarily. 'Oh, and what's that?'

'We could always play strip poker.'

6

'Strip poker?' Sorrel stared at him, aghast. 'Oh, no. Certainly not.'

In her confusion, she half rose from the table, but his hand slid across to clamp on hers.

'So you really are chicken,' he taunted. 'A yellow chicken.'

'No, I'm not,' she retorted hotly. 'It's just that . . . '

But her protests tailed away. Why not? After all the humiliations he'd inflicted on her, wasn't this her chance to get her own back? She'd strip him to his briefs — or maybe even less — then, still fully dressed, she'd get up from the table and walk away with supreme indifference. A macho man like Matt would find that very hard to take . . .

'All right.' She met his opaque green eyes full-on. 'If you really want to. We'll have to start off with more clothes on, though.'

'Of course.' His gaze flicked over her bikini. 'It would be a pity for the game to be over too soon, wouldn't it? Wait here.'

As the green mesh door swung to behind him Sorrel felt a hysterical laugh bubble in her. Was she crazy — playing strip poker, of all games, with this man? No, she wasn't, she told herself resolutely. She'd wipe the floor with him.

When he came back, he had added to his cut-off denims a pair of old black espadrilles, a black vest, an olive sleeveless combat jacket — very suitable, Sorrel thought, with a touch of Matt's own brand of sardonic humour — and a battered straw hat. He was carrying a navy shirt, white jeans and a pair of flip-flops, which he dropped into her lap.

'Put these on. And in case you can't count, they make us exactly equal.'

'But I'd rather wear my own things,' she said tightly.

'What's the matter?' In the shadow cast by the overhanging vines, his eyes gleamed like pale emeralds. 'Afraid of my clothes as well as of me?'

No, not afraid, actually — just terrified. Of anything to do with you.

Without a word she stood up and, not looking in his direction, reached for the shirt. It was soft and silky, and as she turned down the collar it smelled faintly of Matt, so that it couldn't have belonged to any other man . . . Hastily she snatched up the white canvas jeans. When she wriggled into them though, they were too tight to zip up, so, conscious of a pair of eyes unashamedly taking in every movement, she thrust her feet into the flip-flops and slid into her chair.

'You've forgotten this.' He reached for a navy yachting cap which had slipped unnoticed to the floor and jammed it on to her head. His eyes were very near hers, but as she swallowed all he said was, 'We have to start off equal, don't we?'

'Of course. Right,' she went on briskly, to quell the mingled trepidation and excitement which were suddenly swishing round in her stomach. 'You deal this time, if you like.'

★ ★ ★

'First game to me, I think.' With a little tingle of triumph, Sorrel laid down her five cards.

'No, it's not,' he protested, pointing down at the table. 'You said five cards in sequence was a winning hand.'

'But yours aren't all the same suit. Look — ' she jabbed with her finger ' — two spades, one club, two hearts. While I've got — '

'OK, OK,' He gave his cards a ferocious scowl, then, looking up, caught the remnants of her faint smile. 'And what's the matter with you?'

'Nothing. I was just thinking — oh, dear, we aren't a very good loser, are we?'

The scowl deepened. 'Maybe we

haven't had much practice at it.'

'Yes, well, we can all learn, can't we?'

She gave him her sweetest smile, then sat back in her chair, watching as he surveyed himself, lips pursed. Finally he slid from his wrist his superb gold watch — as he set it down she glimpsed the Gucci insignia on its dial.

'But I haven't got a watch,' she exclaimed. 'That's not fair.'

He rolled his eyes. 'You English, with your *fairness*. All right, I'll take off my hat, then. No, wait.'

Pushing back his chair, he got up and went off into the house again, coming back this time holding something cupped in his palm.

'Keep still.'

Before she could move he caught up her left hand and slid a silver ring first on to her middle finger and then, when that was too loose, down on to her thumb.

'Satisfied?'

She studied the wide band of cold metal encircling her thumb, twisting it slightly so that the disc caught the light. It did not carry his initials, as she had expected, but a superbly incised profile — hooked nose, thin lips frozen in a cruel grimace.

'What is it?' She looked down at it with a stirring unease.

'Oh, an ancient Toltec deity — the god of war, I think. It's genuine — very old. I bought it in Mexico City and had it made into a ring. Now — ' he dropped into his seat ' — your turn to deal, I think.'

'Yes.'

Sorrel reached forward to gather the cards together and began to shuffle them. The ring was heavy on her hand, so that not for a second could she forget it was there. Matt's ring — that pitiless face mirroring the ruthlessness she so often glimpsed in him.

She dealt the cards then picked up her own, keeping her face deadpan as she saw the two aces . . .

★   ★   ★

'Another game to you?' Matt slapped down his cards.

'Afraid so. You really shouldn't have discarded that king of hearts.'

'Now she tells me. Ah, well.'

With a resigned shrug, Matt came to his feet. Unzipping his cut-offs, he stepped gracefully out of them, folded them, and dropped them neatly into the crown of the straw hat which lay on the floor beside him. It left that superb body naked, except for the black silk briefs slung low across his narrow hips.

She tried to look away, but something stronger than herself drew her eyes, fixing them to that slash of flimsy silk, which did almost nothing to hide his intense masculinity. Her breathing was growing rapid and shallow, until she was dizzy, almost hyperventilating, the sweat trickling down her back.

'Shall we go on, then?'

Dragging herself out of the sensual miasma, she saw, through eyes that were wide and drowsy, Matt sliding back into his chair.

'Oh, but — '

With a huge effort she roused herself. Something had gone wrong; she knew it. She was beating him hollow, and yet there wasn't any of the triumph which she'd been looking forward to. In fact, somehow, very subtly, while losing all down the line and reduced to a sliver of silk underwear, he was still in charge. It was she who, quite suddenly, wanted to call a halt.

Head bent, she fidgeted with his ring. When she'd lost that one game — well, with a hand like that, even Paul Newman would have thrown in his chips — and she'd begun taking off the ring, he'd stretched out a lazy hand and put it over hers. 'Leave it,' he'd said. And he'd tweaked off her cap and dropped it on the floor.

Now she cleared her throat. 'Look — we won't go on. I — I don't mind, honestly.'

'Thanks, but I wouldn't dream of it.' He gave her a smile which she could not quite fathom, then gestured to his body, all but naked. 'After all, I got myself into this mess, didn't I?'

'Yes, but — '

'No buts.' He silenced her with an imperious wave of the hand. 'My deal.' And he gathered up the cards . . .

* * *

She lost that game easily. She couldn't blame the hand — a good one, with four diamonds. No, it was quite simply that sitting opposite Matt as he leaned casually back in his chair, his bare chest and shoulders gleaming like satin in the early evening sun, her concentration was being insidiously eaten away. And, even more than that, under the mega-voltage power of his personality she was all at once beginning to feel that she was the beginner in this particular poker game.

Without a word she kicked off one of her flip-flops and began to shuffle the cards, trying to use the simple, rhythmic action to suppress the panic which was suddenly rising in her . . .

Matt was still in his briefs. She, though, was down to his ring — and her bikini. The panic had become full-blown now, but this time, when she picked up her cards and saw the superb hand chance had given her, it subsided. Weak with relief, she laid down the cards — four aces and the five of spades.

He leaned over, peering at them. 'Very good. But surely — ' and before Sorrel's horrified gaze he slowly spread out a consecutive run of hearts ' — a royal flush beats four aces every time?'

She stared at his cards in utter disbelief, then forced her eyes up to his.

'How do you know it's called a royal flush?' Ugly suspicions were flaring in her mind. 'I haven't told you that.'

'Yes, well . . . ' Matt leaned back in his chair again. 'It's all coming back to me now,' he said blandly.

'What do you mean, coming back to you?' Sorrel heard her voice, shrill and angry. 'So you *have* played before.'

He spread his hands deprecatingly. 'Oh, not since my college days.'

She gave a brittle laugh. 'So you — '

'Yes.' He smiled reminiscently. 'I seem to remember a few hands of poker a week paid my fees at the Harvard Business School.'

'You lied to me. You said you couldn't play cards.' Her voice was shaking.

'Correction. My precise words were: They bore me. They do — but it seems they have their uses.'

'You let me win. All those games.' Her voice was still trembling. 'They were just a charade.'

'Isn't the whole game a charade — getting one up on your opponent?'

'I suppose so,' she muttered.

'Well, I'm waiting.' All at once there was a steel edge to that husky purr. 'You lost, remember?'

Sorrel ran the tip of her tongue round her lips, which were suddenly most cracking with dryness.

'All right, damn you.' She went to

take off his ring, but again he stopped her.

'I told you, leave it.'

In the fading light their gazes locked as the tension wreathed itself around them, almost suffocating her.

'But — ' She swallowed, then blurted out, 'I'm not playing any more.'

He gave an unpleasant laugh. 'Sweetheart, who's playing?'

She leapt to her feet, the chair clattering to the floor, but he was too quick for her. Seizing her round the waist as she struggled frantically, he pulled her into his arms.

'L-let me go,' she panted, almost sobbing with anger and fear.

'Not yet, my sweet. I haven't quite finished with you.'

'I said — '

But the rest of her words were lost as his mouth took hers in a savage kiss. There was no finesse, none of the skilled seduction of the accomplished lover, yet the sheer violence of his lips and tongue as they plundered her

mouth, bruising her soft flesh, tore out of her the most basic physical response as her body twined with his, burning skin against burning skin.

She moaned, and felt her hips moving against his in the age-old gesture of female invitation and submission. Her fingers clenched on his bare back, the nails cutting into his flesh, and as his lips slid down over her throat she arched her neck, her eyes closing, as her breath thundered in her ears and a roaring tide of fire swept her along.

Dimly she became aware of Matt's fingers at her back, and then her breasts were free for his hands and mouth to stroke, caress, suckle, until they throbbed under his touch. When his teeth caught the nipples, taking them up, nipping them, an exquisite agony shafted through her as her mind and body came to the brink of no return.

'Oh, Matt — please.' She gave a broken sigh but then, next moment, he released her just as violently as he had taken hold of her.

167

'Sorrel.' She opened her dazed eyes, still heavy with desire, to see him smiling down at her — the same cruel, taunting smile of the face on his ring. 'Next time, my sweet — ' incredibly, his voice was perfectly controlled — those wild, searing moments, when the sexual passion buried deep inside her had flared, had left *him* utterly unmoved ' — maybe you'll be more careful who you play cards with — and who you set out to humiliate.'

So he'd realised that, too. Skilled predator that he was, he'd laid his snare with consummate cunning — and she'd walked right into it. As her face crumpled he caught her by the shoulders and shook her.

'Well? Do you hear me?'

'Y-yes.' Her whole frame was trembling, so that she could hardly get out the single word.

He held up her bikini top. 'Game to me, I think. Just one more to go.'

'No!' It was wrenched out of her.

'So I was right — a chicken and a

cheat.' And he spread his hands wide in sneering dismissal.

There was no smile on his lips now, no desire either — no human warmth of any kind. Just the ice-cold triumph of the conqueror who, out of contempt — not pity — had finally released his vanquished foe.

Biting fiercely on her inner mouth, still swollen from his assault, Sorrel felt the warm blood ooze out. She dragged the silver ring from her finger and it fell with a clatter on to the wooden boards. Then, snatching the bikini from him, she turned and blundered down the veranda steps in the direction of the beach, his light, mocking laugh pursuing her.

7

'Tell me one thing, will you? Just how much longer are we going to be here?'

Matt, who had apparently been engrossed all through breakfast in the current half-yearly report on the General Agreement on Tariff and Trade — she'd finally managed to decipher the title upside-down — looked up. His eyes were hidden by the dark glasses and she could make out nothing of his expression. All she could see was her own taut face, reflected in those twin lenses.

'I've told you,' he replied coldly, 'I have no idea. I am not in radio-telephone contact with my yacht, and I'm not a clairvoyant. Sorry.' He turned back to his report.

'But surely,' she persisted stubbornly, 'men like del Castillo and Laborde can't just drop out of circulation for

170

long without people asking awkward questions.'

He gave a faint shrug. 'Ricardo's a friend of mine, so there's no problem about him being on my yacht. As for del Castillo, it's been spread around that he's taken himself off for a rest-cure in a health clinic in — where is it? — oh, yes — ' he smiled faintly to himself ' — the Swiss Alps.'

'But — '

'And with his lifestyle, that's a pretty credible story for people to swallow. So I'm sorry, my sweet, but the talks can go on for quite a while yet.'

'Quite a while? You mean weeks — months — years?'

Sorrel, feeling her veneer of brittle composure splinter at the edges, leapt to her feet and, snatching up the breakfast things, retreated to the kitchen.

She shot the china into a bowl then stood, her hands gripping on the sink, breathing deeply until she had regained enough control to begin washing up, her hands working mechanically, her mind rehashing yet again the scenes of the previous evening.

As soon as she'd reached the beach she'd flung herself into the water, cutting fiercely through the waves in a despairing attempt to blot out the memory of that mocking laugh and more — much more — the taste and smell of Matt, which had still filled her body.

It had failed, of course, as she'd known it would, but when she had finally returned through the darkness to the house, Matt had already eaten and had shut himself away in the tiny office. So she'd made a cheese sandwich and forced it down, slumped on one of the kitchen stools, then had taken herself off to her sofa-bed.

When, much later, he had come into the sitting-room he had not spoken, but she'd sensed his dark shadow pass across her tightly closed lids. As his bedroom door had closed, though, to her horror, she had felt slow tears sliding down her face and, still weeping silently, had drifted off to sleep . . .

Up-ending the washing-up bowl, she dried her hands, then used the cloth to mop her brow. Heavens, how sultry it was this morning. No breath of wind stirred the shrubs outside, which were already hanging their wilting heads, and when she looked up at the sky the blue had given way to a yellow brassy glare. Victoria had told her that it was coming up to the rainy season — maybe there was going to be a violent electric storm. Certainly it felt as if the air, laden and heavy with static, was holding its breath — waiting for something.

Or maybe it was just inside her, the feeling that a storm was about to break over her head. Last night Matt had been intent on punishing her for her pathetic attempt at escape. He'd humiliated her, then let her go.

But surely she wouldn't get through today without him carrying on with his sport. He'd promised — no, threatened — that he would make love to her, and he wasn't a man to make a threat and not carry it out. And, when he did move in for the kill, would she be able to fight back? For how long could she hold out against that desire which surged through her with the power of a spring tide whenever she was near him?

Back on the veranda, he was just getting up from the table. Forcing herself to walk right up to him, she said defiantly, 'Look, I can't just sit here all day. I'm going for a walk.'

He nodded. 'OK, I'll come with you.'

But that wasn't what she'd meant — and he knew it, of course.

As he pulled on a navy singlet, tucking it into his denim shorts, she snapped, 'Oh, of course, I forgot — you daren't let me out of your sight. I'm amazed you haven't chained me to your desk-leg.'

'Don't think that tempting thought hasn't crossed my mind,' he replied grimly. 'But it's too hot to work this morning, so I'll show you round the cay.'

'But — '

'Yes?' He glanced up from thrusting his feet into a pair of espadrilles — those same black espadrilles that he'd worn last night.

'Oh, nothing.' She could hardly tell him that she was terrified of being with him — and far more terrified of her body's unthinking response to him in this lushly sensual paradise. He sensed it anyway — she saw that in the sardonic glint in his eye . . .

On the beach, she kicked off her sandals and picked them up.

'How is that cut on your foot?' It was the first time that he had spoken.

'Fine, thanks.'

They were like two strangers, she thought sadly — walking along the beach, a yard of creamy sand between them. No — worse than strangers, they were enemies, with a universe of distrust and contempt dividing them.

A trickle of fresh water threaded its way through the sand to the sea, and Sorrel dipped a toe in it.

'Ugh, it's cold.' She turned, smiling unthinkingly, but at his aloof expression the smile faded. 'If you'd rather go back — ' she began.

But he ignored her invitation. 'The stream rises in the higher ground over there. Come, I'll show you.'

He struck off through the tangle of undergrowth behind the beach, leaving her to follow up the steep terrain. As she struggled to keep up with him the sweat trickled down her neck, and she ran a finger inside the collar of her pink cotton shirt to ease it away for coolness.

Then, ahead, she saw Matt halt in a clearing encircled by misty blue jacaranda trees and scarlet flamboyants. A spring of clear water bubbled out from among some mossy chunks of limestone rock, trickled down over some rocky ledges then widened out to form a small pool, edged by luxuriant tropical ferns. On the far side an overgrown frangipani hung over the clear water, dropping its creamy blossoms to float in drifts across the surface. Their heady perfume filled the hot, still air until the whole clearing was redolent with it.

It was a perfect spot, heart-wrenchingly perfect, and Sorrel felt her throat tighten painfully at its sheer beauty.

'Well? What do you think of it?' Matt, thumbs jammed in the belt of his denim shorts, lounged up against the trunk of a flamboyant, watching her.

'It's lovely,' she said huskily, and turned away so that he would not see the weak tears shimmering in her eyes. 'Is — is it natural?'

'The spring is, of course, but according to the real-estate guy in Bridgetown, who sold this place to me, the pool and the clearing were made by the previous owner — a Country and Western star from the States.'

'Really?' Sorrel laughed — the first natural laugh she'd managed for what seemed a lifetime. 'Who?'

He gave a disparaging shrug. 'No one I'd ever heard of. He bought the cay as a honeymoon surprise for his new bride and — well, maybe this spot held particularly happy memories.' He gave her a slanted glance. 'Anyway, he had the place landscaped for her.'

'I see.' In her mind's eye, Sorrel saw those newly-weds lying twined on the grassy bank just at her feet, the shadows softly dappling their bodies, and the familiar knife-edge twisted in her heart. 'How romantic,' she said softly.

Matt's mouth gave a cynical twist. 'Sorry to disappoint you — but not really. When I came along he was selling the cay to finance the divorce package.'

'I see.' That soft-focus image in Sorrel's mind shattered.

'Disappointed?'

'Perhaps — but hardly surprised.' Her tone matched his. 'After all, that's how love always ends, isn't it, Matt?'

She looked full at him, but he had turned away and was reaching up to pull down the branch of a tree. It was loaded with large orange-coloured fruits, which glowed like molten gold among the glossy leaves. He snapped off half a dozen, tossing them on to the ground, then one more, which he handed to her.

'Thanks.' She looked down at it. 'A ripe orange straight from the tree — that's a new experience.'

'It isn't an orange. It's an ortanique — a superior sort of cross between an orange and a tangerine.'

Dropping down on to the bank, he took one of the fruits and began peeling back the rough skin, then glanced up, to see her still standing uncertainly.

'Sit here.' He patted the grass imperiously, and after a tiny hesitation she sank down beside him. He handed her the peeled ortanique. 'Here — you have this one.'

Their fingertips met, Matt's warm and alive with that strange vibrancy which always ran through his body, and she drew back quickly to concentrate every iota of attention on the fruit. Even so, she could not prevent herself from casting sneaky glances as he neatly peeled another, then divided the golden sweetly scented segments and ate them one after another.

He had taken off his sunglasses, and beside his eyes she could see the tiny white crease-lines fanning out. How black his lashes were — and how long. Longer than hers — longer than any macho man's had any right to be, she thought with a wry little twinge — and when he lowered his gaze they almost swept his cheekbones.

His eyes hooded suddenly, and, realising that he was perfectly aware of her watching him, she hastily bent forward, dabbling her sticky fingers in the water, delightfully cool after the clammy heat.

'If you fancy a swim, it's deep enough. I often bathe here.' Matt was lounging back on his elbow, a blade of grass between his teeth.

'No, thank you.' Her voice was constrained. 'I haven't got my swimsuit on.' As he very well knew.

'Oh, but we're all broad-minded on this cay,' he said in a lazy drawl.

'Some of us, perhaps,' she said tightly.

'Please yourself.' Reaching for another fruit, he peeled it. 'Want half?'

She was going to refuse, but they were so delicious. With a muttered 'Thanks' she took it, the juice spurting out on to her hand and down over her thigh in a sticky golden trail.

As she sat back something pricked her calf, and she scratched at it absently with her fingernail. Next instant though, glancing down, she gave a gasp of shock as she saw a continuous line of small red ants racing up her leg. She swatted at them and then, as there was a vicious nip on her wrist, realised that others were swarming all over her arm.

'What are they?' She was scrambling to her feet.

'Pepper ants.' Matt too had leapt up, and was slapping at his own leg. 'The ground's alive with the bloody things. The fruit must have brought them out.'

'Ouch!' Sorrel gave a yelp then hit out wildly at her stomach. 'They're in my clothes.'

He grabbed hold of her loose blouse, dragging it up. 'Keep still. I'll get them off you.'

But, beside herself now, she turned to run.

'Where the hell are you going?'

'I'm getting out of here, of course.'

'Don't be a fool. They're all over you — us.'

He winced, and rubbed fiercely at the back of his own neck, then, before she'd realised what he was going to do, he flung his arm roughly round her waist and dragged her headlong into the pool with him. They both hit the water face-down, and Sorrel, all the breath knocked out of her, went right under.

Matt came to his feet first and, putting his hands under her arms, hauled her to the surface. Her hair was plastered to her face, water blinded her and she clutched at him for support, coughing and choking.

'Are you OK?'

Sorrel nodded, quite unable to speak, as he tilted her chin and wiped away the clinging strands of hair.

'Sorry about that.' But through her blurred gaze she saw that his green eyes were alight with devilment. 'I've heard of ants in the pants, but this is ridiculous.'

Her mouth twitched, then they both simultaneously broke into peals of helpless laughter, clinging to each other as the sound of their mirth echoed around the clearing.

'I *told* you — ' she was gasping for breath ' — I didn't want a swim. But you never take any notice, do you?'

'Not often, no.'

He was still laughing down at her, but as she laughed back all at once her heart lurched heavily against her ribs. Here — right now — with his black hair lacquered to his skull, water streaming down his face and chest, her physical desire for him was all but unbearable. But more, so much more than that . . . As she stood waist-deep in this island pool time slipped away, and he was that other Matt whom she had loved so deeply. And whom she loved still.

Unbidden, the knowledge — the dreadful certainty — crashed like a tidal wave through the defences she had so painfully erected against it. The laughter was wiped from her lips and for endless moments all she could do was clutch on to him, gazing blindly up into his face. Then, with a small incoherent sound which was almost a sob, she wrenched herself free and, blind with panic, went to wade out.

He caught her up in the shallows, swinging her round to him. 'Hey! What's the hurry? Now we're here, let's have that swim.'

'Oh, n-no. I want to get out.'

'To give our little red friends their second course, you mean?'

He lifted a hand, delicately picked off a frangipani petal from her cheek and tossed it back into the pool. He was still smiling down at her, but suddenly the smile vanished from his eyes and they went very dark. As she followed his gaze she realised with a gasp of horror that her soaking clothes, clinging to her body, were all but transparent. Through the pink blouse and white shorts her cotton bra and briefs showed clearly, and in turn they revealed the distinct outline of her breasts and rosy nipples, and the dusky crescent of hair above the apex of her thighs.

Against all conscious volition her gaze went back to him, and she saw that his clothes too — the navy singlet, the denim shorts — had moulded themselves to him, accentuating the intense maleness of him.

Next moment he had reached for her, dragging her into his arms. His mouth came down on hers and she felt the fierce hunger in his lips and the answering greed in her own, as their bodies, despite the chill of the water, were all at once on fire with the intense heat which blazed between them.

Matt moved to pull her out on to the far bank, but when she stumbled they both fell to their knees in the shallows.

As his arms tightened round her she slid her hands under his singlet, marvelling yet again at the play of muscles beneath her fingers. His mouth and hand fastened on her breast, cupping then nuzzling it through the wet cotton and she closed her eyes against the erotic friction of his hot palm as her body was racked by an intense shudder.

'Oh, my sweet, I must have you now.' Matt's voice was harsh with passion.

'Yes, yes. Oh, yes,' she murmured, locking her fingers in his dark hair to press him to her breast.

Lifting her into his arms, he carried her out of the pool and laid her on the grass. His hands fumbled urgently at the sodden waistband of her shorts, then she felt the zip begin to give and they were sliding down her thighs, being pulled free. He buried his face in her belly, his lips scorching her navel, and as she writhed beneath him his fingers slid inside her panties. But then, in the very same instant as she tensed to raise her hips slightly to help him ease them away, one tiny part of her reeling brain clicked into gear.

What was she doing? Couldn't she see beyond this fleeting moment of passion? Carlos and the launch could come tomorrow — today, even — and Matt would walk away from her, contemptuously tossing her her freedom while leaving her chained to him forever.

She loved him — she wanted him. Every aching part of her being yearned to abandon itself to him as he took her in his arms and made love to her, wildly, passionately. But remember the pain you suffered last time, that minute portion of her mind told her. Remember the months, the years of misery. This is the man who all but destroyed you once — and if you're fool enough to let him break your heart a second time, you'll *never* put the pieces back together again.

'No!' Her face blank with fear, she tried to push him away. 'No, I don't want — '

'Yes.' He clapped his hand over her mouth. 'Yes, you do.'

His face was dark with desire, the pupils of his eyes very black and intense, as though they focused not on her, Sorrel, but on his prey. That feral look appalled her. She sucked in her breath to scream but his hand trapped the sound as he came down on her in a dreadful re-enactment of that other near-violation.

Her eyes were those of a helpless creature, blank and staring, as she stopped struggling and lay supine, quite unable to resist him. But it was that look of sheer terror which saved her. For next moment he had jack-knifed to his feet and stood looking down at her, his mouth a tight slash in his face.

'Don't cringe away like that.' His voice was thick, his breathing unsteady. 'I have no intention of taking you by force. I didn't rape you last time, and I don't aim to now.'

As she gazed up at him he went on remorselessly, 'But you're not going to hold out against me much longer; I promise you that.' His thin lips twisted. 'Surely even you can see that the sooner we both slake this thirst we have for each other's bodies, the sooner it's over and we're cured forever.'

Out at sea thunder growled like a frustrated predator, making her flinch.

'Don't worry about that, either — it's miles away,' he said curtly. 'So you can stay here if you want to. I'm going back to the house.'

He turned away and she raised herself up to watch, a dull, aching pain under her ribs, as he went lightly off between the trees. Within seconds he was lost in their shadows, and she sank back on the soft grass, sitting there huddled for a long time, staring at nothing.

Finally, though, she became aware of a bedraggled pepper ant, struggling to climb up a frond of fern which dipped into the pool just beside her. She lifted it out and looked down at it lying in her palm.

'I'm sorry,' she whispered, then set it down on the grass and watched it lurch safely away.

✗ ★ ★ ★

For the hundredth time, Sorrel leapt up and paced the veranda — up and down, up and down. This evening the strange restlessness in her which would not let her be still for five minutes was somehow the exact antithesis of the sultry air that hung heavy over the cay. There was something almost menacing in it, and in the soft rumbles of thunder which had prowled around the cay all afternoon, and which came again now.

She went through to the kitchen, and when she came back out into the sitting-room there was a sliver of light from under the office door. Matt had been in there when she'd got back and was obviously staying all day, she thought dully. She should have been grateful that he'd shut himself away from her, but instead she found herself longing to be there with him, just watching him as he worked.

Out on the veranda again, she stopped at his window and looked in through the half-open louvres. He was sitting at his desk, facing her, and in the harsh light of the angled lamp his features looked drawn, the lines even more deeply etched. With a finger of one hand he was punching out numbers on a calculator, and scribbling on a sheet of paper with the other.

After several minutes he paused, passing his hand wearily across his brow. That simple gesture made Sorrel ache to rush in, take him in her arms and cradle him to her. A vice-like pain closed over her heart and she shut her eyes, rocking on her feet as its full force surged through her then slowly ebbed away.

Five years ago, she'd loved him — but it had been the first love of a young girl, dazzled by a handsome face and Latin charm. Now she knew Matt, saw him clear-eyed for what he was — a harsh, unfeeling man, who drove himself unsparingly — yet still she loved him, and with a woman's love, which was far more dangerous. Like a moth, fluttering too near a naked flame, she hovered by the window, feasting her eyes on him.

'What do you want?' He looked up at her through the shutters, so abruptly that she had no chance to melt into the shadows. 'Well?'

'I — I was just going to say dinner's ready,' she stammered.

'I'm not hungry. I'll make myself a salad later.'

'Please yourself.' The tension was snapping in her voice. 'I've only spent two hours getting it, but I'll throw the lot away. Maybe the tree frogs will appreciate it.'

'Oh, for God's sake.' He hurled down his pen and came to his feet so fast that even though there were the shutters between them she retreated a pace. 'Just serve it up, will you?'

When he came out on the veranda

she was already seated at the pine table, her fingers plucking restlessly at her olive-green linen skirt. As he slid into the chair opposite she saw that he too had at least taken the trouble to change, into ash-grey casual trousers and a white open-neck shirt. His face, though, was no different, except that that morose, brooding look had intensified even more.

With no more than a grunt, he picked up his fork, squeezed the lime segments over the wafer-thin slices of smoked salmon and the fan of avocado which she had arranged on the plates, and began to eat.

When she brought in the main course he had poured the white wine she had chosen, and as he drained his glass he glanced briefly at the contents of the pottery dish.

'Chicken pieces and peppers in a sweet and sour sauce — all from your store cupboard,' she added defensively.

'Hmm. And since when did you learn to cook? I seem to remember beans on toast were the height of your culinary ambitions at one time.'

Sorrel stared at him, her sapphire eyes dark. What thoughts lay behind those caustic words? Did he have any regrets? No, of course he didn't — regrets were for weak fools like her.

She forced a careless laugh. 'They were — but then Ben asked me to do some entertaining for him.'

'I bet he did.' His tone was unmistakably hostile, but she ignored the provocation.

'Yes. He was hoping to impress some potential clients, so I decided I ought to take a few lessons. Is that enough rice for you?' But her bright tone did nothing to dissipate the brittle tensions that were in the air all around them.

'If you're so valuable to him, I'm astonished he lets you out of his sight.'

'What's that supposed to mean?' Sorrel felt her face grow warm.

'It's not *supposed* to mean anything,' he replied evenly. 'But in any case, he's coming out at the end of next week to that apartment he so generously loaned you, isn't he? Isn't he?' he demanded, as she sat in stunned silence. So he knew that, too. Just how much more had he found out about her?

Finally, though, she managed a shrug. 'You obviously know he is.'

'I do hope you'll be back in time.' His lips curled. 'We'd hate Ben to be disappointed, wouldn't we?'

'Oh.' Sorrel gave a gasp, in which anger and pain were evenly mixed. 'I've already told you, Ben is my business partner — full stop.'

'If you say so.'

'Yes, I do,' she retorted hotly. 'And it's a pity your spy didn't also tell you that he'll be bringing Nadine, James, Philip and Tom with him.'

'Quite a little party you have lined up.' There was no mistaking the innuendo. 'No wonder you're so desperate to get back there. Such a pity for you to miss out on the fun.'

'I don't have to take this from you.'

She leapt to her feet, the fury fizzing in her now.

'Honey, you have to take anything I care to give you.' His voice was steel-honed with menace. 'Sit down.'

Their gazes locked and then, despising herself for her weakness, she slid reluctantly back into her chair.

'For your information,' she went on frigidly, 'Nadine is Ben's wife and the boys are their two-year-old triplets. They happen to be the reason that Ben asked me to do some client hostessing — Nadine's permanently exhausted these days.'

'Indeed?' His tone was still subtly barbed.

'And — not that it's any business of yours — ' her voice was rising again ' — she and Ben are ecstatically happy.' Just for a moment, at the thought of that happiness, she felt a little stab of jealousy. 'Whereas I have no intention of ever allowing any man to mean a single thing to me.' And, setting her head proudly, she returned to her meal.

* * *

Matt finished off his iced chocolate mousse — which she'd hurriedly snatched out of the freezer cabinet — then, getting to his feet, picked up his coffee-cup.

'Thank you for the meal,' he said formally. 'But if you'll excuse me, I want to get on.'

She heard his office door close, a cold little click which shut her out. Just as he would always shut her out, she thought miserably. Her coffee was bitter on her tongue, and, crossing to the veranda rail, she stood for several minutes gazing into the darkness, then emptied the cup into the hibiscus bushes and began to gather the dishes. All at once, though, as she felt the black depression enveloping her, she set them down again and ran swiftly down the steps.

At the edge of the sea she walked the length of the beach, back and forth, back and forth, her feet sinking slightly in the wet sand. After the stillness of the day a wind had got up, and although there was no moon the sky was just light enough for her to see the white-crested waves breaking on the reef. Far out on the horizon lightning, silver-white, flickered incessantly, but any rumbles of thunder were drowned in the surging waves.

She'd half expected Matt to follow her, but then, there was no need, was there? No passing yachtsmen — or even fishermen — would be out tonight. And there could be no other possible reason why he should want to be with her.

She was turning back for the house at last when she saw something glimmering palely among the trees. Then Matt, still in his white shirt and grey trousers, appeared and she stopped dead, waiting for him to come up to her.

'What the hell are you *doing*?' His voice was crackling with irritability.

'Nothing.' She turned away, but he caught her by the wrist.

'Don't you realise it's past midnight, you little fool?'

'So?' She jerked free. 'There's no need for you to wait up for me, you know. I'm a big girl now.'

'I thought you just might have been crazy enough to go for a swim. After all, night bathing is one of your specialities, isn't it?' In the darkness he put out a hand and touched her hair. 'Dry. So you weren't that crazy, after all.' He looked past her at the surging waves. 'Now that I'm here, though, I think I will.'

'Oh, but — '

'I need something to clear my head.'

After dragging off his shirt he stepped out of his trousers, so that he was in just his black briefs.

'It's very rough further out,' Sorrel began again tentatively. 'I've been watching the surf breaking . . . '

But he grinned down at her, his teeth very white.

'I enjoy a battle.' And, turning, he waded out through the shallows, a faint gleam of light on his back and shoulders.

Sorrel watched his dark head, his arms cleaving a path through the churning water, then lost him in a turmoil of boiling spray. She stood, gnawing her lip, her eyes strained to the line of foaming water until they were gritty with salt. He was a strong swimmer, his limbs sleek as any seal's, but out at the reef four thousand miles of ocean were pounding remorselessly down on anything that dared to bar its way.

If he should drown out there . . . Pressing her knuckles to her mouth, to still the whimper that was rising in her, she began pacing to and fro. After a few more days — or less — the launch would come and she'd never see Matt again. But she would always need to know that he was alive. How could she get through every day of the rest of her life if she wasn't certain that somewhere on this planet — maybe even sparing her a fleeting, careless thought — a living flesh and blood Matt existed?

A jagged line of breakers were racing

in towards her, very fast, the white horses which surmounted them rearing and plunging. And then, quite suddenly, the moon came out from behind a ridge of midnight-black cloud. Its cold light glinted on the thundering waves — and among them she saw Matt.

The intense joy and relief welling up in her made Sorrel's knees all but buckle under her. He was riding those wild sea-horses — they were bringing him in to her. Scarcely aware of what she was doing, she walked out into the sea to meet him, arms outstretched. As they came together in the surging shallows he took her in his arms, and she melted into her dream.

8

For endless moments he held her to him, the water rippling round them both, but then, as a wave broke over their thighs without a word he drew her out on to the sand. His body was icy-cold, yet burning with the intensity of the fire within, and when he kissed her she felt the heat blaze up between them, white-hot.

There was no tenderness, building to slow desire. Lost in her erotic dream, she moaned with frustration as he put her from him, but only to drag her clear of her clothes. She felt the zip of her skirt break as he tugged it from her, then the tiny pearl buttons on her blouse were torn away as he pulled that off too.

The moonlight gleamed on his wet chest and shoulders like a film of silk. Her hands were reaching out to him, exulting in the contrast of smooth skin and crisp hairs, and in the feel of the two tiny peaks of his nipples which throbbed under her palm. His own fingers trembling with urgency, he wrenched open the catch of her bra, cupping his hands to receive her full breasts as they came free. Then his mouth was scorching the tender flesh moulded in his grasp.

Overwhelmed by her need for him, Sorrel staggered and almost fell, but he caught her, then laid her down on the sand. He moved over her and she pulled him down to her, her thighs parting to receive him as he slid his hands beneath her buttocks to raise her hips against his thrust. There was pain, fierce and tearing, so that for a moment she gripped his back, her nails scoring the skin. But then it was past as, caught up in the incandescent fires which flared between them — far brighter than the flickering lightning — their bodies melded into one.

Her whole frame tightened in ecstasy,

her hips arched against him, and then, as she cried out wordless, incoherent sounds, which were lost in the waves which roared around them and in her brain, his body tensed like a bow. She felt herself filled with his warmth, sweet as honey; they both shuddered and lay still . . .

★ ★ ★

When she roused, a huge bank of violet clouds was blotting out the moon again. Dazed, she lay staring up at that opaque mass, then, as memory flooded into her, she swivelled her head sharply. Matt was lying on his side, his head propped on his elbow, watching her. His face was shadowed, so that she could make out none of the features; all she could feel was his breath, warm on her skin.

For a moment he seemed a stranger — remote, aloof — and her heart, already fluttering crazily, jumped a beat. But then, taking her hand, he raised it to his lips and gently kissed the palm.

'Hi,' he said softly.

'Hi.' She hardly dared to speak, for fear that all her aching love for him would spill into her voice.

Instead, her fingers twined with his and he gripped them hard. The silken water was lapping around their bodies; it was warm, but Sorrel shivered suddenly and, getting to his feet, Matt stooped and gathered her to him.

She lay, encircled by his arms, her head against his chest, feeling every beat of his heart against her cheek, and that strange sensation that was half intense pain, half bubbling joy seized her. What would tomorrow bring? Only the pain. But tonight she would live for the joy of loving Matt and giving him pleasure.

On the veranda, he halted and looked down at her, his eyes very dark and sombre.

'You know,' he said huskily, half to himself, 'I had forgotten just how lovely you are. Tonight, lying in my arms, you look just as you did five years ago.'

His hungry gaze roved over the soft lines and curves of her naked limbs, then she felt his whole body go rigid, and in his horrified eyes she saw the stark realisation of what he had done.

'Sorrel?' His voice was anguished.

'What?'

He buried his face in her hair. 'Why didn't you tell me that you were a virgin? Oh, God, how I must have hurt you.'

'Well . . . ' She hesitated. 'Just a little.'

'Why the hell didn't you stop me?'

'I didn't think you'd believe me,' she whispered.

'Oh, my sweet.'

'And besides — '

'Yes?' he said tautly.

'I — I didn't want you to stop.' Her voice was almost inaudible, but he heard, and his arms tightened around her until she all but cried out.

His face pale and set, he carried her

through to the tiny bathroom, put her down in the shower cubicle and set the water running. Taking a tablet of soap, he gently sponged her all over, starting with her neck and shoulders, then on across her breasts and finally, going down on his haunches in front of her, he soothed away all the soreness.

When he went to switch off the jets she caught his hand and said shyly, 'Please — let me do the same for you.'

Without a word, he handed her the sponge, and she began caressing his body with it, tentatively at first, over his shoulders and arms, then with increasing confidence, long, sensuous strokes on his belly and legs as she too knelt before him.

As she moved upwards to his inner thighs she felt the violent kick of desire in his body, then, as though unable to wait a second longer, he took the sponge from her and tossed it aside. Lifting her to her feet, he swung her into his arms again and carried her into his bedroom, shouldering open the door.

'But we're dripping wet — we'll mess up the sheets,' she protested as nervous laughter bubbled in her throat.

'Damn the sheets.'

He set her down very carefully, as if she were made of fragile glass, then stood looking down at her as she lay, her limbs a delicate gold against the cream silk sheet and flushed with rose from the bedside lamp, her wet hair tangled on the pillow.

'You look like a beautiful mermaid that I've just trawled up from the depths of the sea,' he murmured throatily. 'Will you swim away at dawn, I wonder?'

'Oh, no, Matt,' she said very softly as she returned his look with a steady gaze. 'I'll stay just as long as you want me.' And no longer, that cold, clear little part of her brain added.

His face, his body, were silhouetted against the lamplight. She lay motionless, watching him come down to her, that dark rider from the waves, then, as he emerged from the shadow, she opened her arms to him.

This time it was different — less a violent, piercing intensity than a slow ravishment of all her senses, as over and over he skilfully brought her body to a state of quivering, frantic expectation. He called from her responses which were so profound that finally, shaken to the very roots of her being, she could only cling helplessly to him, her eyes wide and unseeing as she cried out his name.

And this time, when at last he possessed himself of her, each of them was at so intense a peak of trembling avidity for the other that almost instantly they were both flung into mindless oblivion.

When the storm abated and they were lying twined in each other's arms, she gazed up at him with slumbrous eyes.

'Will it always be like that?' Her voice shook slightly at the potent memory.

He took her hand and kissed each finger in turn, before he looked at her over them, his eyes glinting.

'You mean for us individually or just when *we* are together — you and I?'

That hateful, sardonic note was back in his voice, but as she winced he muttered under his breath and drew her closer.

'Don't look like that, my sweet. Surely you know me well enough to understand that I always take refuge in cynicism when I am feeling most deeply.' His lips gave a wry twist. 'I hate to admit it, *querida*, but it has never been like that for me before.'

'Good.'

She gave him a shimmering smile, turned her head into his shoulder and fell into a deep sleep . . .

*   *   *

When at last she stirred and opened her eyes, the room was filled with a pale, luminous wash of colour. Dawn. Matt

210

lay beside her, his cheek cradled in one hand, his long lashes shading his cheekbones. All the lines of strain had gone — he looked younger. Five years younger, she thought, with a poignant twist of her heartstrings.

Lifting her hand, she very gently brushed the tip of one finger across his lips. He murmured something, then flung himself over on to his other side, his dark head nestling into the pillow.

Sliding out from under the sheet, Sorrel caught up his robe and went out on to the veranda. She stood, knotting the robe and gazing around her. Surely never in the entire history of the world had there been such a morning, she thought, as her heightened senses drank it in. Such a sky of pale apricot, such a vivid intensity of colour in the pink and red hibiscus, in the dazzling emerald of a lone humming-bird which was sucking the nectar from the morning glory vine over her head.

She hugged her arms to her, as if she could hug the morning, and vowed silently, If I live to be a hundred, I shall never forget this moment. She knew now that she would bear the wound of loving Matt for the rest of her life, that that was the price — but it was a price she would gladly pay.

Matt. She turned back towards the door, unable to stay away from him any longer, then saw through a cleft in the screen of oleanders, way out on the horizon, the dot of a boat. Of course, it could be any boat, heading any-where . . .

She stood looking at it for a long moment, a tight hand gripping her chest, then very slowly she went back through to the bedroom. Matt, twined in the sheet, was still asleep. She gazed down at him a moment longer, trying to imprint his features on her mind forever, then, kneeling beside him, kissed his brow.

He woke instantly, his green eyes as alert as a cat's, then as he saw her he smiled lazily and, lifting his hand, gave a lock of her hair a soft tug.

'Good morning.'

'Matt,' she said unsteadily, 'the launch is coming.'

'Ah.' He grimaced, then nodded slightly. 'Are you sure?'

'Yes. Quite sure.'

'How far away?'

'Oh.' She gave a faint shrug. 'A long way out, but — '

'In that case — '

He grinned wickedly at her, then, without warning, reached across and pulled her on to the bed beside him. There was no time for subtlety. Caught up in instant, flaring desire, there was a wild, almost pagan quality to the way they took one another's bodies, as though for each of them there could be no tomorrow.

* * *

Sorrel, shattered into a million fragments, lay motionless until, in the outermost orbit of her consciousness, she registered a soft footfall on the veranda. Matt heard it too, for as she stiffened his arms tightened round her. But then, as they both caught a discreet knock on the mesh door, he gently loosed her, kissed her soundlessly, then put a finger to her lips.

Sliding out of bed, he picked up the robe from where it lay in a heap on the floor, put it on and went out of the room, knotting the tie as he did so. She heard him greet someone, then Carlos's voice in reply. For a few seconds she lay on the bed, half listening to their conversation, her body languorous from Matt's lovemaking, her mind still drifting on that other sensual plane of existence.

Finally, though, the real world claimed her once more. It was over — she didn't need Matt to come and tell her that they were leaving. Her fantasy had belonged to the night; now, the daylight blotted it out. Tears burned her eyes. How cruel that her joy should be so short-lived — just one night of love in Matt's arms, and then the launch — and harsh reality — had come. But at least she had this one night to treasure through the long years ahead.

She got to her feet and went through to the bathroom. In the mirror a stranger's face — another Sorrel Eliott, face flushed, eyes heavy, the wide mouth swollen and pouting — gazed back at her. And when she looked down at her body somehow that, too, had indefinably changed where Matt's hands had roamed, sliding over her warm skin, caressing, rousing her eager flesh, imprinting on her the scent that belonged to him alone.

Her arms cradling her breasts, she stood, eyes closed, until it seemed as if he still held her. Here, last night, they had showered together, locked in each other's arms. If she showered now she would lose that feel, that smell . . . Opening her eyes, she turned the jets full on and stepped under the cascade of water.

Back in the bedroom, she pulled on

the first things she came to — a peach-coloured polo shirt and a peach and white cotton skirt. Then, very methodically, she began taking the rest of her clothes from the wardrobe and laying them in her case, folding them with extreme care, as if it was all at once overwhelmingly important that they were not even slightly creased.

When she had finished, she stooped down to make sure that nothing — not even the cheapest T-shirt — had slipped off its hanger to join that silk, Sakkara-perfumed blouse still lying in the far corner. But, after all, you're no different from that other woman, are you? her inner voice whispered. Less glamorous and sophisticated, maybe, but just as ephemeral for Matt Ramirez.

She was closing the lid of her case when he came back.

'I've made coffee. Would you like some?'

'No, thank you. I'm not thirsty.'

When she smiled her face felt stiff, but Matt wouldn't notice — she knew that. He was already subtly different, as though a part of him wasn't in the room, preoccupied — with matters she could never have any part in.

'Have the talks gone well?' She had to force herself to ask.

'Yes — yes, they have. They have finally hammered out an agreement which should save both them and my country. So, yes — ' he smiled, and for a moment she had his full attention ' — the talks have gone well.'

'I'm so glad for you, Matt.'

Impulsively she took his hand in hers. He looked down, then raised her fingers to his lips to give them a fleeting kiss.

'I'll take this through, then grab my own things.' He picked up her case, then glanced back at her perfunctorily. 'You're looking very beautiful this morning, *querida*.'

But she knew he hardly saw her. She ached for him to take her in his arms, hold her close, whisper the endearments that had made her pulses leap with rapture through their one, brief night. Instead, she merely smiled, took her shoulder-bag from the bed and walked out to the veranda, where Carlos was drinking coffee . . .

★   ★   ★

The launch cut its motor and pulled alongside the jetty. At the far end of the beach was the headland where she had sunbathed and seen the men come down to the boat. How long ago? Was it really just four days? As they had passed the marina, minutes before, Matt had pointed out his yacht, already at anchor, sleek and gleaming white in the morning sun. Those steps running down the side — she'd hauled herself up them, not knowing that her heart was about to be broken all over again.

'She's beautiful,' she said, in a dead little voice, and then, as she picked out the letters on the stern. '*Ariadne.*'

'Maybe I should change it to Sorrel — a much better name for such a lovely boat. What do you think?' He smiled down at her, and the pain twisted inside her like a knife-thrust.

'I shouldn't,' she replied steadily. 'I don't think Sorrel's a very good name for a yacht.'

He shrugged. 'We'll see.'

And then he went to stand by Carlos, his fingers drumming a tattoo on the brass rail in his impatience to be back.

He helped her out, then went on up the steps which led from the jetty, Carlos following with her case. They went through a high wrought-iron gate, past a tangle of tall, scarlet-leaved poinsettias, then emerged on to a lawn running up to the most gorgeous villa Sorrel had ever seen.

It was a low, sprawling building in the pretty, pinkish local coral-stone, over-looking the sea through a line of casuarina trees. She just had time to glimpse a jade-tiled pool at one side, half hidden by a white, fretted stone screen over which tumbled a huge stephanotis, its waxy flowers scenting the still air, before Matt mounted the grassy steps two at a time, then turned on the terrace to wait for her.

'Carlos will take you back to your apartment. Ricardo is here, and soon I must go to the yacht to see del Castillo before he flies out this afternoon. So — goodbye for now.'

'Matt — ' she began.

'What is it?'

There was the faintest frown of irritation between his finely arched brows. Of course. She mustn't make a fuss, must she? That wasn't how Matt liked his women to behave. He was already politely, gently — ruthlessly — disengaging himself from her, and she must do the same.

'Nothing — except goodbye.'

Nailing that stiff smile on to her mouth again, she held out her hand. He took it and held it between his for a moment.

'So, you see, I shall be occupied this morning, but as soon as I can . . . ' He left the sentence unfinished.

'Of course, Matt. And don't worry, I

quite understand.' She forced another unreal smile, until her face felt as though it was cracking, and then, when he was already turning away, she looked back at Carlos. 'I'm ready . . . '

She saw nothing of the vibrant colour and beauty of the island during the drive. Cushioned in the luxurious leather upholstery of the red Bentley Continental, she stared out, unseeing, only rousing herself as the car slid to a halt by her apartment. Carlos opened her door, then lifted her case from the boot and went to carry it in, but she took it from him.

'Thank you. I can manage.'

She answered his smart salute with a dazzling smile, then turned away.

The apartment was cool and dark. Sorrel opened a shutter in the kitchen, made herself a cup of coffee and carried it out to the small patio. The guests next door were having breakfast on their terrace, though she couldn't see them. Of course, the girls from Prince Edward Island had been flying home yesterday

. . . She was sorry to have missed them.

The new couple, she gathered, while trying hard not to listen, were on their honeymoon. She heard the man say, 'Now, Mrs Barry, we've been married two whole days and you've forgotten already that I like brown sugar on my grapefruit. How do you suggest I make sure you remember in future?'

There was a giggle, then a scuffle, then silence . . .

Sorrel pressed her lips together until they were numb as the vicious pain struck home beneath her ribs. Maybe once a heart had been broken, she thought dispassionately, like a piece of brittle old porcelain, it was never quite as good again. A week ago she'd been so sure that she was over Matt for good, but now it seemed that those hairline cracks in her heart had been waiting for five years for this moment, to reopen in a raw, bleeding wound.

He wasn't coming — she knew that. He would be 'occupied' all the time now. His life certainly didn't include her — in fact, as soon as he had seen the two men, he would probably jet off too.

A plane had just taken off from the airport. She watched its steep ascent, the fuselage glinting in the brilliant sunlight, leaving a trail of white haze behind it. Not that one, or the next, but perhaps the next would be taking him away . . .

Well, she wouldn't wait around to see. She still had a week of her holiday left, but there was plenty to do back at the office, and maybe it would suit Ben and Nadine to come out here a few days earlier.

Pushing her cold coffee aside, she leapt impulsively to her feet. In the kitchen she picked up the phone and asked to be put through to the British Airways desk . . .

★   ★   ★

Sorrel was just putting her passport in her bag when the taxi arrived. She heard the spurt of gravel under the wheels, then the slam of a door and Victoria's raised voice.

Victoria. Her pinched features broke into a wry little smile. When she'd arrived for work the maid had been bubbling over with pleasure at seeing her, but her sly teasing as to where Sorrel could possibly have been — and whom she could possibly have been with — was more than her bruised spirit had been able to bear. She'd cut her short, told her that she was flying out at midday, then abruptly turned away and shut herself in her bedroom to pack, leaving the maid's pretty face creased with concern.

Now, she opened her purse, took out a banknote and folded it, ready to slip into the girl's hand as a leaving gift, then rezipped her bag with a jerky movement and picked it up. Behind her, the door opened.

'Miss Sorrel — '

'Yes, it's all right, thank you, Victoria.' She did not turn. 'I heard the taxi. Would you please ask the driver to — ?'

'Ask him yourself!'

The snarl in the familiar voice made her spin round, her breath all but slammed out of her. In the doorway, behind the maid, she saw Matt, a thunderous scowl on his saturnine face.

'Where the hell do you think you're going?'

'I — I've changed my flight. I'm leaving this morning.'

'Like hell you are.'

As he advanced threateningly into the room she took a step back, but still somehow managed a defiant glare.

'And who's going to stop me?'

'I am.'

Savagely he hurled the gorgeous bouquet of creamy orchids that he was carrying on to a chair, from where it crashed to the floor, the cellophane crackling loudly. Victoria, wide-eyed, darted to retrieve it.

'Beautiful flowers,' she remarked, to no one in particular, adding, as she retreated through the door, 'I'll put them in water for you, miss.'

'Thank you.' Sorrel spoke automatically, not taking her eyes off Matt. He *had* come. The mingled joy and pain filled her, so that she could barely speak.

'Well?' His scowl deepened. 'Perhaps you would be good enough to tell me exactly what is going on? I turn my back for a couple of hours, and get here to find you on the point of leaving.'

'Yes.' It was all that her dry mouth could manage.

'For God's sake — what do you mean, 'yes'?' He came right up to her, gripping her by the shoulders, his fingers digging deep, and stared down into her face.

'It — it was kind of you to come and — '

'Kind?' He frowned slightly as if in puzzlement. 'I'm never kind.'

'But we both know it's over — and I thought it was better to . . . ' Her voice tailed away, lost in the almost overwhelming longing to lift her hand and tenderly stroke his beloved face.

'Better to sneak off without a word?' he finished grimly. 'Well, for your information, it isn't over. In fact, it's only just begun.'

'Wh — what do you mean?' A wild, unreasoning hope was fluttering like a humming-bird's wings in her chest.

'What I mean is . . . ' He tilted her face to his, and at the sudden tenderness in his eyes that fluttering bird went crazy. 'What I mean is, my darling, that I love you — and I'm going to marry you.'

9

'Marry!'

'That's what I said.' His voice was still crackling with barely pent up irritability. 'What's the matter with you today — are you deaf as well as stupid?' He ran his fingers through his dishevelled hair. 'Sorry. I guess I'm slightly overwrought, but for heaven's sake say something.'

Sorrel, her sapphire eyes enormous with shock, bit her lip. To go from bleak despair to such happiness was mind-blowing. It was like opening a door in a desolate, grey wilderness and finding herself in a world filled with tropical sunshine.

'What do you want me to say?' she asked slowly.

'On second thoughts, don't say anything. No — ' As she went to interrupt him he swept on imperiously.

'I don't want your answer now — you're obviously not thinking straight. And besides, I intend to do everything correctly from now on — I'm going to woo you in the good old-fashioned way.'

'But surely you've already won me.' She managed a slanting smile from under her lashes.

'Don't look at me like that.' His grip tightened as he pulled her against his hard body, then, just as abruptly, he thrust her away from him. 'No.'

He pushed her to arm's length, as if he did not quite trust himself, then held her by her slender wrists. 'I mean it — I'm going to woo you. And then, this time next week, I'll ask you for your answer. And, talking of wooing — ' he glanced down at his watch ' — I've booked a table for lunch at Sandy Lane.'

'Sandy Lane?' she echoed. That dazzlingly opulent hotel, one of the most expensive in the entire Caribbean?

She'd read about it in the brochures but . . .

'Why? Would you prefer the Royal Pavilion?'

'Oh, no. Sandy Lane will be fine.' She glanced ruefully from her simple navy linen dress to his casually expensive white shirt and pale grey silk suit. 'Except that I haven't anything suitable to wear. They won't let me over the doormat in this chain store dress, I'm sure.'

He scowled, then said, with that touch of superb arrogance which always made the hair on her neck prickle, 'Of course they will. You're with me, aren't you? In any case, you look perfect as you are.' And all at once the adoration in his eyes made her want to weep. 'But if it worries you this afternoon I'll buy you a whole new wardrobe. Now what's the matter?'

She gave a slightly shaken laugh. 'Oh, nothing. It's just that I'm not used to being — wooed by a seriously wealthy man.'

'Oh, but you'll get used to it in time, I'm sure,' he replied, deadpan, then his expression changed and, lifting her hand, he pressed his lips to the palm. 'My heart,' he murmured huskily, 'how I love you.'

*　*　*

Orchids . . . pink carnations . . . velvety dark red roses . . . The bouquets arrived every morning, each one more sumptuous than the previous day's, until finally Victoria ran out of vases — and rapturous exclamations. There was lunch at the Paradise Beach and the Sandpiper . . . dinner on the terrace of the Coral Reef Club, the Caribbean shushing softly almost at their feet, fireflies glinting emerald fire in the shadows, and Matt's face, so handsome in the candlelight, his green eyes so tender . . .

That first afternoon he'd swept her from the Sandy Lane dining-room into the hotel's boutique and — ignoring all her remonstrances — bought her enough stunning clothes to overflow the back seat of his Bentley. He'd added set upon set of lingerie in fragile silk and satin, hand-trimmed with lace, and dismissed her blushing protests with, 'They can be for your trousseau. That is,' he had added, with a sideways smile, 'if you decide to marry *me*, of course. No other guy gets to see you in those things.'

As the flimsy, cobweb-soft bras and panties, teddies and nighties had been folded in white tissue, she'd looked at him as he'd leaned against the counter and thought, Marry you? There's not much doubt about that, my darling.

She was aching with love for him, feverish and trembling, as though she had a virus, not quite aware of anything that was going on around her — and certainly not of the ground beneath her feet. Only Matt, to her, was reality.

And when, each evening, he delivered her back to her apartment, it was he who broke from their kisses, thrusting her away from him, even though she sensed the hunger, the impatience in his body. Just last night, when they'd got back very late from the Coral Reef, he'd taken her in his arms, but then, as she'd melted into his embrace, he'd pushed her away, gripping her hands until she had almost cried out. He had said tightly, 'For heaven's sake — go,' and all but shoved her out of the car.

She went into the bathroom and, still dazed with love — and two glasses of champagne — leaned against the wash-basin, gazing at her reflection. It was there, in her face, in her eyes, that naked emotion — her love for Matt. She looked defenceless, somehow, and very vulnerable, and as she stared into those wide dark blue eyes a qualm went through her.

Maybe — surely — it was dangerous to love someone as much as she did. But there was nothing to be afraid of now; the days of wooing were over, and tomorrow Matt would ask her to marry him.

He'd already said, earlier that evening, 'Where — just supposing you *do* say yes — ' he'd given her another slanting grin ' — do you want to be married? They lay on marvellous weddings right here in Barbados, you know.'

She'd hesitated, picturing a wedding on this lovely tropical island, but then she'd said, 'If you don't mind, Matt, I think I'd like to be married in London, with my family and friends.'

'And what about a honeymoon? Mexico? The Seychelles?'

'Your cay — that would be the perfect place. At least — ' She hesitated, biting her lip.

'At least?' he prompted.

'Matt . . . ' Instead of meeting his eye, she began picking at one of the buttons on his cream shirt, but then the words came out in a rush, 'You know that silk blouse I found in the corner of your wardrobe, well — '

'Ah, yes.' Matt's face was deadpan. 'Celia is a sweetie, but she's very forgetful.'

'Celia?' she faltered.

'Oh, don't look like that, my love.' Taking her hand, he crushed it between his. 'She is the devoted wife of Eduardo, my second-in-command. I lent them the cay as a tenth wedding anniversary gift.'

'But that day when I found it, I thought — ' She broke off.

'Yes, I know what you thought.' Matt grinned at her smugly.

'And you let me believe it, and go on believing it,' she added unsteadily, and felt the hairs stir on her neck. There was that hint of latent cruelty in him once more.

'Yes, I did.' His smile faded abruptly. 'My darling, I wanted you to suffer the torments of jealousy, just as I was at the thought of any other man coming near you.'

'Oh, Matt, there was no need.' She looked up at him, tears glinting in the darkness. 'There's never been any other man for me — and there never will be.'

'And no other woman for me.' His

eyes were wholly serious now. 'For five years, whenever I've tried to blot you out by forming another relationship — and God knows I've tried hard enough — it just hasn't worked.' He gave her a crooked little smile, then went on, 'So, the cay it is — always supposing that the owner figures in your honeymoon plans, of course. And if you tire of the simple life I can set up a Caribbean cruise, just for two. What do you say to that?'

'Mmm, that would be marvellous.' A smile curved her soft mouth.

'And afterwards, *querida*, where would you like to live?' He looked at her tenderly. 'I'll keep this place, of course, but would you prefer England?'

'I don't mind where I am, just so long as I'm with you.' Overwhelmed with her love for him, she reached up to kiss his cheek. 'And I'm sure you really need to be based in Tierranueva.'

'Well, perhaps. And I do have a villa there, near the coast — quite large enough for a family.' Their eyes met, and she blushed. 'But we'll keep the apartment in London for when we go across to Europe.'

Now, Sorrel yawned, gave a lazy stretch, then sat up on the padded lounger and looked down at her body. Against her new shiny chocolate-brown bikini, her skin was turning a delicious gold. As she was rubbing in more suntan oil on her stomach and legs Jorge appeared, carrying a tray with a jug of iced lime juice and a bowl of red-gold mangoes which he set down beside her.

She smiled at him. '*Gracias*, Jorge. Er — *es muy bueno*,' she added carefully, practising the Spanish which Matt was teaching her.

The manservant nodded gravely. '*De nada, señorita.*'

'Er — ' She pulled a rueful face, and lapsed into English. 'Have you taken Señor Ramirez a drink? I think he could do with one.'

'Of course, *señorita.*'

They exchanged meaningful glances

as the sound of a computer keyboard being angrily thumped drifted out from Matt's office, then Jorge turned and went back into the pink villa.

Sorrel lay watching him from under the brim of her straw hat. The immaculate servant to his fingertips, he was far too discreet to have shown the slightest reaction to her sudden reappearance in Matt's life but, just as five years ago, he seemed to take pleasure in pampering her. He must have heard her say to Matt how much she adored mangoes, and now no drink ever came without a bowl of the gorgeous fruit, each looking as if it had been lovingly hand-polished in the kitchen.

She poured herself a drink, the ice in the frosty jug chinking softly, and, after peeling a glossy-skinned fruit she sank her teeth into its scented flesh. Dropping the stone on the plate, she dabbled her sticky fingers in the blue water of the pool, letting it lap her hand like warm silk. Mmm. Maybe she'd have another swim — or maybe, half-asleep in this beautiful garden of Matt's, she was just too lazy to move.

The keyboard clatterings ceased abruptly, and next moment Matt pushed open the glass door and came storming out to stand over her, scowling darkly.

'Something wrong?' she asked tentatively.

'Of course there's something wrong,' he snarled. 'The damn thing's given up on me.'

'I'm not surprised, the way you were treating it. But surely,' she went on hastily, as his scowl became even more ferocious, 'there must be a computer agency in Bridgetown. They'll send someone out straight away.'

'Straight away isn't soon enough — I want it fixed right now. So, what are you waiting for?'

'Me?' Sorrel shrank back further into the lounger. 'Oh, no, I couldn't possibly — '

'Rubbish. You're a computer trouble-shooter, aren't you?'

'No. I just — '

'Come on. I haven't got all day.' And, reaching down, he pulled her to her feet.

She followed him across the terrace, her foot-steps dragging, and into the office. She had been very careful not to come in here during the last few days; now she looked around in open astonishment at the state-of-the-art communications equipment set up along all four walls — data transmission facilities, including telex and fax machines, a bank of TV screens, set up presumably for teleconferencing rather than viewing the latest rerun of $M^*A^*S^*H$, and, on a desk taking up nearly the whole of one wall, an entire management work-station, including a very sad-looking computer, its screen totally blank.

Sorrel ran the tip of her tongue round her dry lips. 'Look, Matt — '

'Well — what are you waiting for?' he demanded. 'There's the user's manual, for what it's worth. Get to work. I'm going for a swim.' And, peeling off his

T-shirt, he disappeared.

She stood motionless for several seconds but then, feeling slightly sick, sat down at the console to inspect the invalid. Oh, she'd worked with machines like this many times — her own was a less expensive version — but even so, to be handling Matt's . . .

And that, of course, was why she'd been so reluctant to come into this room — and why now her usually nimble fingers were so stiff and awkward. The last time she'd sat before one of Matt's computers her entire world had collapsed around her, and now she felt an almost superstitious dread that the wounds which had only just healed were about to be ripped open again.

Yet surely not. Last time Matt had *thought* he loved her — now she *knew* that he did. So therefore he must trust her . . . An intelligent man like Matt could have no difficulty in running what was, after all, a perfectly straight-forward computer terminal . . . Could it possibly be that he'd set this up deliberately — to show her, in his own way, that after all the suspicion and disbelief he trusted her absolutely?

As the little glow flickered in her, then burst into joyful flame, she turned back to the keyboard and was instantly totally immersed in the challenge of restoring the machine to full health once more . . .

★ ★ ★

She straightened up, flexing her shoulder muscles, then, pushing back her chair, went outside. Matt was sprawled face-down on a lounger in the shade of the pergola. She stood for a moment, her eyes feasting on that superbly honed body, and then, as though sensing her gaze warm on his skin, he raised his head.

'Well?'

'The file-names didn't match up.'

'I know that,' he said irritably.

'You must have specified the wrong

drive.' Her eyes held his for an instant. 'But it's all right now — I've fixed it.'

'Great.' He leapt to his feet, smiling broadly. 'Good girl — I knew I could count on you.'

Her heart overflowing with gratitude, she stood on tiptoe and kissed him. 'Thank you, Matt,' she said huskily.

'What for?'

'Just — thank you.'

'Right. I'll get back to it, then.'

'Oh, give yourself a break first. You look tired.' She put a hand on his arm. 'You haven't had that swim yet, have you? Come on, let's have a swim. I'll beat you to the far end of the pool.'

'OK, sweetie. You're a bad influence, though — you know that?' he said mock-severely, 'But then I'll have to leave you, anyway. I've got an appointment in town in under an hour. You stay on here — it's Jorge's afternoon off, but he'll fix you lunch before he goes.'

'No, I think I'll go back to the apartment and have a rest. Can you drop me off when you go?'

'Sure.'

'Thank you.' She smiled ruefully. 'All these late nights are catching up on me.'

'Me too.' He pulled a wry face. 'But when you're wooing the most beautiful — ' he kissed one eyebrow ' — the most desirable — ' he kissed the other brow ' — young woman in the western hemisphere — well, sacrifices have to be made.'

Colouring with pleasure, she turned away to the pool, but as she stood poised on the edge he went on laconically, 'And on the subject of wooing — just in case you're wondering — I haven't forgotten that the time is up for your reply. Wear something special tonight, *amada mia*. I'm planning a celebration meal — at least — ' he gave her a teasing look ' — I hope I'll have something to celebrate. Now — what was that about beating me? Honey, you have absolutely no chance.'

And in one fluid movement he was

diving in and cleaving his way towards the far end, so that when she arrived he was waiting, grinning in triumph. He pulled her against him and kissed her hard, their wet limbs twining in the aquamarine water.

When they finally pulled apart he looked down at her, gently brushing her lips with his fingertip.

'Oh, my sweet, if you knew how much I love you.' He gave a shaken laugh. 'But I'll still wait for tonight for your answer.'

★ ★ ★

The slam of a car door roused her from a pleasant doze. She rolled over, the smile still lingering on her lips, then came wide awake as she heard rapid footsteps followed by Matt's voice. Heavens! She let out a little wail. She must have slept for hours. He'd arrived to take her out to dinner and she hadn't even washed her hair, or finally made up her mind whether to wear the black silk dress or the —

Her bedroom door opened and Matt stood there, framed against the brilliant sunlight. He paused in the doorway, trying to focus in the shuttered darkness, then closed the door behind him and came across to stand looking down at her.

'Hi. You're early,' she said softly, and held out her hand to him, but he did not appear to see it.

'Well, well. So you're still here.'

Still here? What did he mean? And that voice . . . Though the words were softly — very softly — spoken, there was something in them which made her whole body tense.

'Strange,' he went on, in that same low tone, 'I half thought you'd have made a run for it by now.'

'I — I don't understand you, Matt.' She lay motionless, staring up at him, her hands clutching on the sheet.

'Don't understand?' The sudden savagery in his voice, after the level quietness, almost made her cry out.

In three strides he crossed to the window and jerked open the shutters, letting the light flood in. Then he turned back, his eyes raking over her body — obviously naked under the single sheet. His lips, already tight, whitened into a thin line, then with a violent gesture he ripped it away.

As she gasped with shock he ground out, 'Get some clothes on.'

Catching up her cotton housecoat, which lay across the bottom of the bed, she dragged it on, her fingers shaking so much that she could scarcely belt it.

'Please, Matt — ' she began unsteadily, forcing herself to meet his furious gaze. 'Tell me what's happened.'

'Oh, God.' He shook his head hard, as if to clear it of some painful memory. 'How can a woman look so beautiful, so innocent, and yet — ' He broke off, then pulled a folded sheet of paper from his jacket pocket. 'Do you know what this is?'

Sorrel took it but, her mind still frozen, she could only stare blankly at the flimsy paper. Finally, though, she looked back at him.

'Of course I do,' she said tautly. 'It's a fax transaction report. But I don't — '

'I'm so glad you don't try to deny it.'

'But why should I?' she asked, bewilderment beginning to merge with fear. 'I handle them often enough in my work.'

'Ah, yes — your work,' he sneered. 'Which do you mean — the official or unofficial variety?' And, when she made no response, he demanded, 'Well, where is it? The original, I mean. And, for your information, a second copy has been sent through to me.'

'A second copy?' As his fists bunched she backed up against the wall, her hands spread against it for support.

'Give it to me, Sorrel.' He jammed his hands into his jacket pockets, but the raw anger was still vibrating in his voice. 'You aren't leaving the island with it — you must see that now — so hand it over.'

'I don't know what you mean. I've

got nothing of yours, I swear it, Matt. Do you really think — ?'

As she broke off, biting her lip, he cut in savagely, 'I've been setting up this deal for months — a merger with a Wall Street bank. My New York lawyers were faxing me the final details today, but when I got back from my meeting nothing had come in, so I rang them. Well, don't you want to know what they said?'

'No. No, I don't,' she said loudly, as the panic began to unleash itself in her.

'They said, my sweet, that a fax, detailing our prospective partner's current financial position down to the last cent, was despatched this morning — at eleven twenty-five, Barbados time.'

'Eleven twenty-five,' she said slowly. 'When I was in your office.'

'Precisely. And, to prove it, they faxed me this copy of the report sheet for the original — ' he waved it in front of her again ' — complete, of course, with time, date and name-code — together with a duplicate, which is now safely stowed away from any greedy, prying eyes.'

Sorrel, her knuckles pressed to her mouth, could only stare at him. Oh, God, it was starting all over again, the nightmare of five years ago. The suspicion, the mistrust, the accusations. And, because she had allowed herself to love him again, she was as utterly helpless against his anger now as she had been that last dreadful time. But, for her own salvation, she had to try to defend herself.

'Are you saying that I engineered the whole thing?' she demanded tightly. 'That I somehow put a jinx on your computer, hoping that you would ask me to put it right, just to have the chance to get hold of any messages that might come through?'

'No, of course not,' he replied harshly. 'But I know you well enough, *querida* — who better? — ' his lips twisted, and again she glimpsed the pain, next second ruthlessly stamped down ' — to be certain that you saw that fax and realised that you'd struck gold again. That information would be priceless to any of that bank's competitors — and you knew it.'

Sorrel closed her eyes, trying desperately to recall the layout of his office.

'Working at that computer,' she said at last, 'I had my back to the fax machine. And the messages just slide out into the tray, so I wouldn't have heard anything.'

'No — but when you'd finished you saw the report, lying there so conveniently, and — with that smart little brain of yours already in overdrive — you seized your chance.'

'Please, Matt — ' she began huskily.

'Please, what?'

'Don't treat me like this. Just a few hours ago, you told me you l-love me. If you really do, you ought to trust me, too.'

'God help me, I do love you.' Without warning, he raised one hand, and, tilting her face to his, gazed down at her, his eyes very sombre. 'But that makes no difference. Oh, I don't say you do these things deliberately — you can't help yourself. It's like an illness. You saw it — so you took it.'

'No.' Her voice was all but inaudible. 'I swear to you that's not true.'

'I demand complete integrity from my staff, my associates — '

'And your wife, I suppose,' she said tautly.

'Especially my wife.' As he released her all the anger seemed to go from him, leaving just an overwhelming sense of regret. 'You must see that, Sorrel. The confidential information that passes through my hands daily could destroy business empires — rock governments, even.' His face tightened with self-contempt. 'I suppose you thought you were safe this time, with me behaving towards you like some besotted adolescent.'

'No, Matt — '

'No wonder you were so anxious not to stay for lunch at the villa. You didn't even want to risk me going back into the office. 'You look tired' — 'Let's have a swim'. That's what you said, wasn't it?'

'You did look tired.' But he hadn't looked the way he looked now — his face pale and set in harsh lines, his lips compressed as though on some vicious inner pain.

'Just give it to me, Sorrel, and I'll let you walk free.'

Out of his life forever . . .

She shook her head. 'I can't give you what I haven't got.' As his hands bunched by his sides again she went on steadily, 'One day, Matt, you'll come to know the truth about me, and I hope you'll be sorry.'

'*Sorry.*' He almost spat out the word. 'Do you think I'm not sorry now? Sorry I ever met you — sorrier still that I let myself fall in love with you twice over, knowing what you are?'

'There's nothing more to be said.' She straightened up, and, picking up her tiny bedside clock, snapped it closed with a sudden violent gesture. 'Before all this you said you were going to propose to me this evening. Well — you're not going to now, of course, but I wouldn't marry you anyway.'

Even though she was slowly bleeding to death inside from the wounds he had inflicted, she set her head proudly. 'I could never marry any man who didn't l-love me — ' just for a moment her voice betrayed her ' — enough to trust me.'

She gave him a sad little smile. 'I don't think you can ever really have loved me, Matt, and at least you've found that out in time. And now I want to pack, so just — just go, will you?'

A terrible dead weight of misery was settling on her, and she longed to be alone.

'I'll call the airport for you, shall I?' he said unpleasantly. 'Book you the first flight out.'

'You needn't bother.' The bitterness overflowed. 'Five years ago, in case you've forgotten, you were generous enough to ring for a cab for me. But I've grown up since then, Matt. I can make my own phone calls now.'

As she went to walk past him, though, he caught hold of her by the wrists, so that she winced with pain.

'I'm letting you go — you realise that? If I were so minded, I could fetch in the police. I could strip this room to locate that fax. But I'm not going to. I promise you one thing, though.' His grip tightened even more. 'And this time round I'll spell it out. If one iota of that information leaks out, I shall know the source, and I will destroy you utterly — professionally, and personally — and take the greatest pleasure in doing so.'

As the door closed behind him she sank on to the bed, her trembling legs unable to hold her upright a moment longer. Her hands hurt. Looking down, she saw, though barely registering it, that her nails had dug into the soft skin of her palms and little pinpricks of blood were oozing up through the grazed skin.

Catching hold of the pillow, she

cradled it in her arms, burying her face in it to stifle the broken whimpers of misery. Destroy her utterly — in the future? But how could he possibly do that, when he'd done it already?

10

England. Sorrel leaned forward, peering down through the tiny rain-flecked window. Back home, back to work tomorrow morning, in a job she loved, blotting out the past so that very soon Matt Ramirez would be even less substantial than these laden grey clouds which the plane was lurching down through.

But then, as though to mock her resolve, one of those spasms of intense despair, which had been shaking her at intervals ever since they had taken off from Barbados, took hold of her again. Leaning back in her seat, she closed her eyes as it shuddered through her again. At Kennedy Airport — in her desperation to be away, she had taken the only available flight, which had been via New York — she'd all but missed the final departure announcement as she'd sat, wrapped in her unhappiness . . .

'Excuse me.'

A hand touched her arm, and she opened her eyes to see the young man in the neighbouring seat bending towards her. He had spent the first half-hour out of New York trying — nicely enough — to chat her up, then given it up as hopeless and buried himself in a book.

'We're supposed to fasten our seat belts,' he went on.

'Oh — sorry.'

Sorrel roused herself, smiled, and fumbled with her belt. This time when she glanced out of the window the airport was below them, and as the plane banked she saw a large Boeing poised ready for take-off as one of the small executive jets which whizzed around Europe came skimming in to land along the runway.

'Are you all right?' Her neighbour was looking at her, concern puckering his roundish, good-natured face.

'I — yes, of course.' She tacked a

258

smile in place — the smile which she was going to have to learn how to use in the weeks ahead — dazzling, but empty.

He grimaced. 'I don't much care for landings myself — not many people do. Look, I don't suppose the bar will be open at this time in the morning, but how about a quick coffee when we get through Customs?'

'Oh, it's very kind, but — '

'Please do. It'll take them some time to stack all the luggage on the coaches.'

'Coaches?' Sorrel's dazed brain picked up the final word. 'Oh, no — I'll be getting the tube in from Heathrow.'

'Heathrow?' The young man looked at her warily, as though he had just discovered that she was crazy. 'But we're not landing there. Didn't you hear the announcement a while back? They've closed all the airports in the south-east of England because of dense fog.'

'Oh.' Roused at last, she clapped a hand to her mouth. 'Where are we landing, then?'

He shrugged. 'Some airport up north. Birmingham — or was it Manchester? It doesn't really matter, does it?'

No, it didn't matter. Nothing *really* mattered, and never would, now that she'd never see Matt again.

It was still raining as they all trooped down the steps towards where the three airport buses were lined up to take them to the terminal. Sorrel shook out her white lightweight mac to slip it over her shoulders, but the belt was tangled, and if she had not been preoccupied with untwisting it she would have seen him earlier.

'Sorrel!'

As her head jerked up she finally saw him, sprinting across the wet tarmac towards their group. She stopped dead, not breathing, and stood staring as around her the crowd jostled in their eagerness to be out of the rain.

Only when it was too late did she rouse herself, as if from a deep sleep. She made a convulsive leap towards the nearest bus, but Matt seized her hand.

'Didn't you hear me calling you?'

She wasn't hallucinating. In the driving rain his dark hair was plastered to his forehead, just as it had been when he came to her out of the sea, but this was no dream — the deep, vibrant voice was his, the hand holding hers was living flesh and blood . . . She stared up at him, totally bereft of speech.

'It's incredible.' He shook his head. 'I've just landed, and here you are. Thank God we were both diverted to the same airport.'

'H-how did you get here?' she stammered.

'Oh — ' He jerked a thumb across at the white executive jet which had rolled to a halt not far away. 'That's mine.'

'But — ' she could still barely form the words ' — what have you come to England for?'

'Excuse me, sir.' An airport policeman and a grey-suited man had silently materialised, one on each side of Matt.

'What is it?' he snapped, his eyes still locked with Sorrel's.

'Immigration Control, sir.'

The grey-suited man put a firm hand on his arm. Matt looked down at it, and she saw a faint frown crease those elegant brows. No one, but no one laid a finger on Matt Ramirez. But then he relaxed slightly. 'Yes, of course. My pilot has the papers — come with me.'

Turning back to her, he raised her fingers to his mouth, kissing their cold tips quickly.

'Sorrel — ' he held her gaze a second more ' — wait for me — please.'

Wait for him — for this man who had cost her so much pain that she would never be whole again? For this man whom she loved? She watched him walk away, then, barely conscious of the dozens of pairs of eyes fixed on her, climbed into the last bus and, as it juddered and began to move, held on to a strap.

Her luggage was among the first off the carousel and she came quickly through Customs, but still he was there ahead of her in the arrivals lounge. When she appeared, he came towards her and took her case.

'Come on.'

'No.' She drew back. 'Please, Matt. I have to get the coach.'

Through the plate glass window she could see several coaches drawn up, and people from her flight already climbing on board.

'Nonsense. I've told them — I'm taking you down to London,' he said peremptorily.

What she ought to say was, No, you're not, and walk away from him — because with this man there would always be pain, and she didn't think she could take any more.

'Matt — ' she began unsteadily, then, as a heavily-set woman cannoned into her from behind, she was sent stumbling against him.

One arm closed round her, drawing her to him protectively. He gave the woman a scowl, which ought to have felled her to the ground, then pulled Sorrel to the edge of the mêlée.

'Look,' he said, 'I've hired a car — it'll be ready in a few minutes. Until then, for heaven's sake, let's go somewhere quieter.'

In the crowded café he found a table for two, and she watched, her chin propped on her hands, as he joined the self-service queue. Even in here he looked cold — he was still wearing the lightweight linen suit and open-necked shirt that he'd changed into for that appointment when he'd dropped her off at her apartment. It seemed light years ago, somehow, not hours — but then she was light years older now.

He set down a tray of coffee and a plate piled with chocolate éclairs. When she looked from them to him, he grimaced.

'I didn't think either of us would fancy bacon and egg, and I seem to remember you went for the éclairs when we had tea at Glitter Bay last week.'

Glitter Bay . . . that afternoon . . . that magical day. They'd spent the morning at Andromeda Gardens, strolling hand in hand among the orchids and brilliantly flowered trees, had a picnic lunch, then swum and slept on a tiny deserted beach that his white mini moke had bounced its way to down an overgrown track, before going on to the hotel for an English afternoon tea . . .

Sorrel bit hard on her inner lip to keep back the treacherous tears that burned behind her eyes.

As Matt slid into the chair opposite she looked up and, really for the first time, they gazed directly at one another. He looked drawn, and in the space of hours new lines had appeared at the corners of those lovely green eyes.

He smiled faintly, as if reading her thoughts, then said abruptly, 'When Jorge came back from his afternoon fishing trip, he told me that after we'd left he'd found a fax in the in-tray and put it safely away.'

'I see,' she said stiffly. A crazy,

unreasoning joy was filling her, but she dared not surrender to it. 'So that means you don't believe any longer that I took it?' She was holding his gaze, her eyes steady.

'Of course it does. It means that I've been the blindest brute who ever — ' He broke off, and, snatching up the coffee-pot, poured two cups, pushing one towards her.

'Thank you.' She added milk, then mechanically lifted the cup to her lips.

'I can only say I'm sorry,' he went on huskily. 'As for Jorge — he sent his apologies too. That was just before I fired him — on the spot.'

'You fired him?' Sorrel set down her cup, so that a few drops of coffee splashed unnoticed over her hand. 'But it wasn't his fault. You know it wasn't,' she added accusingly. 'He was just looking after your interests.'

'Yes, well — maybe,' he grunted sourly. 'And maybe I was a little hasty. Oh, don't cry, *querida*.' Her tears shimmered. 'If I call him when we get to my flat in London he'll hardly have started packing. I'll offer him a generous bonus to stay on.' He gave a wry grimace. 'He's been with me for ten years, and I've already been asking myself how I'd possibly manage without him. Will that suit you?'

Her taut face relaxed for an instant. 'Yes — thank you. But — ' she took a deep breath ' — I'm sorry, Matt, I'm not coming back to your flat.'

'Because of — ?' His lips tightened.

'Last time?' Her gaze met his again. 'No, not that. But you must see — there's no future for us.'

It was so very hard saying those words, with a pair of beautiful green eyes fixed on her, just inches away, but she must. 'Oh, you know now that I'm innocent — and I hope you know that I was that other time. I was foolish, but I didn't intend you any harm. But it changes nothing. Something else, at some time in the future, will make you doubt me — suspect me all over again.'

'But I know now that I love you,' he

exclaimed, then ran his fingers through his hair. 'Although I was too proud to admit it to myself, I really did love you five years ago, and I never stopped loving you — though I told myself often enough that I had. And then, when you were dragged into my cabin like a half-drowned mermaid — ' he raised his hand and tenderly stroked her hair ' — I couldn't bear to let you go again. Oh, I could have clapped you in irons — ' he gave a half-smile ' — or held you under lock and key at my villa, but I had to keep you just to myself, on my cay.'

'Oh, Matt.' Her eyes brimmed with tears again. 'Yes, I think you do love me — and I love you. But that doubt — it will always be there, between us. And bit by bit it will push us apart. No, please — ' She stopped him as he went to interrupt. 'You said it yourself — you demand absolute integrity from everyone around you, and especially from your wife. Sooner or later, I would see the suspicion in your eyes, and it would break my heart.'

'Sorrel — my darling.' He took her hands — still cold in spite of the hot coffee — and held them as she tried to draw back. 'I know I don't deserve you. I shall never deserve you,' he added unsteadily. 'But I cannot — will not — give you up. I love you too much — you must believe me.'

'I do believe you, Matt, but — '

'Even when I *did* think you were guilty, I realised I couldn't let you go. I came back to your apartment, then, when a highly abusive Victoria — ' he rolled his eyes at the memory ' — informed me that you'd gone, I chased you to the airport. I arrived just as your flight took off. *No* — ' he held up his hand as she tried to break in ' — it's my turn now. When Jorge came back with his afternoon's catch, I'd already contacted my pilot and was sorting out my papers to follow you — or even, with you going via New York, get in ahead of you. Which I managed — just.'

That bubble of happiness was swelling inside her, but still it mustn't take her over.

'You love me, Matt,' she said, very softly, 'but still you didn't believe me. And I have too much pride — '

'*Amada mia*.' His fingers tightened on her hands. 'I swear I shall never, ever mistrust you again. And, if you'll only let me, I shall spend the rest of my life proving it to you.'

A group of ebullient teenagers sat down nearby, dragging two tables together, and Matt pulled a face then leapt to his feet.

'Let's get out of here. We'll stop for breakfast on the way down to London, if you want to.'

Putting a hand on her elbow, he lifted her out of her chair, then, taking her case, steered her outside to where a sleek grey Jaguar was waiting, a uniformed chauffeur beside it. Matt stopped dead, a few paces away.

'Sorrel — ' He turned her to him, speaking urgently. 'I can't wait till we get to London. Please forgive me. Without you, my life, my work, my wealth — they're nothing — just ashes in my mouth. Marry me. *Marry me*, my darling, and I promise you, by everything that's in my power, you will never regret it.' He gazed down at her, his face strained with tension.

How much she loved him . . . Strange, she hadn't realised until this moment just how very much.

She held out her hands to him. 'Matt.'

It was all there in the luminous smile she gave him and in that one simple word — all her intense love and longing for him. And, as the chauffeur studied his polished toecaps, with a little sigh she went into his arms.

★   ★   ★

'Happy, my love?'

Matt spoke very softly into her hair, and Sorrel, her cheek nestled against his bare chest, could only smile. 'Mmm.'

'Sure?' There was that faint note of uncertainty in his voice again, which plucked at her heartstrings.

'Perfectly — ' turning her head a fraction, she pressed her lips to his warm skin ' — absolutely sure — for all my life.'

'Oh, my darling.'

As Matt's arms tightened around her she rested her hand on his — her left hand, with the superb sapphire ring and — since yesterday morning — the plain gold band, which was far more precious to her.

He put her gently away from him, so that he could look at her. From far across the Caribbean, the setting sun turned their faces to molten gold as they stared into one another's eyes, drinking in the love and adoration each saw there.

'*Querida*.' Matt's features twisted suddenly. 'I love you so much. But it's true — I do not deserve you.'

'Of course you do.' She caressed his cheek.

'No.' He shook his head. 'But at least you already know your husband's faults. I shall just have to spend the next fifty years showing you all my good qualities.'

'Oh.' She looked up at him, her face solemn, though an impish gleam lurked behind the wide-eyed innocence. 'But I only married you for your faults. I didn't realise you *had* any good qualities.'

'Well, you little — '

As he made a grab at her she wriggled out of his grasp, jumped down the veranda steps and raced towards the sea.

But as she reached the edge of the beach he caught hold of her silk sarong, which was tied under her arms. Her laughter turned to a squeal as, snatching her up, he carried her across the sand to the water's edge, then waded in until he was knee-deep.

'Shall I throw you in?' In the dusk, his eyes were glinting wickedly.

'No — no,' she wailed, torn between

terror and laughter. 'You'll ruin my beautiful sarong.'

'In that case . . . ' he let her slide down his body until she was standing locked against him ' . . . I'd better take it off, hadn't I?'

And, peeling the clinging silk away from her, so that she was naked, he hurled it in the direction of the sand.

He was laughing, but as he looked down at her, taking in the pale, tangled hair round her shoulders and her slender, lissom form, she heard his breath catch.

'How lovely you are,' he said throatily. 'So lovely that I half think you're a dream that I'll hold in my arms all night, and then at dawn you'll vanish.'

'Oh, no, Matt.' Her mouth curved tenderly. 'I'll never go away.'

Far out, the sea was thundering on the reef, the waves curling towards the shore as the white horses of foam tossed their heads. Matt drew her to him, and she closed her eyes as his lips found hers. The sea, the beach, the breaking waves, the silver moon above — all this had been just a dream, a fantasy. But now she held her dream in her arms — warm, loving, *alive*. And, sleeping or waking, it would never leave her.

THE END

We do hope that you have enjoyed reading this large print book.

Did you know that all of our titles are available for purchase?

We publish a wide range of high quality large print books including:
Romances, Mysteries, Classics
General Fiction
Non Fiction and Westerns

Special interest titles available in large print are:
The Little Oxford Dictionary
Music Book, Song Book
Hymn Book, Service Book

Also available from us courtesy of Oxford University Press:
Young Readers' Dictionary
(large print edition)
Young Readers' Thesaurus
(large print edition)

For further information or a free brochure, please contact us at:
Ulverscroft Large Print Books Ltd.,
The Green, Bradgate Road, Anstey,
Leicester, LE7 7FU, England.
Tel: (00 44) **0116 236 4325**
Fax: (00 44) **0116 234 0205**

LOOKING FOR LOVE

Zelma Falkiner

Fleur's sweetheart, Tom, disappeared after being conscripted into the Army during the Vietnam War. Twenty years later, Fleur finds a package of his unread letters, intercepted and hidden by her widowed mother. From them, she learns that he felt betrayed by her silence. Dismayed, but determined to explain, Fleur engages Lucas, a private investigator, to help in the search that takes them to Vietnam. Will she find Tom there and put right the wrong?

RELUCTANT DESIRE

Kay Gregory

Laura was furious. It was bad enough having to share her home with a stranger for a month — but being forced to live under the same roof as the notorious Adam Veryan . . . His midnight-dark eyes challenged Laura to forget about her fiancé Rodney, and she knew instinctively that Adam would be a dangerous, disruptive presence in her life. She'd be a fool to surrender her heart to such careless custody . . . but could she resist Adam's flirtatious charm?

CHANCE ENCOUNTER

Shirley Heaton

When her fiancé cancels their forth-coming wedding, Sophie books a holiday in Spain to overcome her disappointment. After wrongly accusing a stranger, Matt, of taking her suitcase at the airport, she is embarrassed to find he is staying at her hotel. When she discovers a mysterious package inside her suitcase, she suspects that the package is linked to him. But then she finds herself falling in love with Matt — and, after a series of mysterious encounters, she is filled with doubts . . .

KIWI SUNSET

Maureen Stephenson

In 1869, dismissed from her employment with Lady Howarth after being falsely accused of stealing, Mairin Houlihan emigrates to New Zealand. There she meets Marcus, the son of Lady Howarth, who had emigrated there to farm sheep. But later, despite her innocence, Mairin is held on remand on suspicion of murder. Marcus tries to help her — but with all the circumstantial evidence against her, how can he? If convicted she will hang. Who had committed this terrible murder?